GW00382586

A FRAC

KEN N. KAMOCHE was born in Kenya. He studied Commerce at
Nairobi University and Management at Oxford where he was a
Rhodes Scholar. Ken is an academic, a journalist and a writer of
fiction. His academic writings are on how to manage people, and
how managers can learn from jazz improvisers. He has worked
previously as an auditor in Kenya, Uganda, Somalia and as an
economist in Poland. He has taught in the UK, Portugal, Australia
and Thailand. For a number of years Ken wrote 'Letter from the
East', a weekly column for a Kenyan paper. He is a regular colum-
nist for Kenyan papers and on www.G21.net. Ken currently lives in
Hong Kong and is completing a novel on the lives of black people
in Asia.

KEN N. KAMOCHE

A FRAGILE HOPE

SALT

CAMBRIDGE

PUBLISHED BY SALT PUBLISHING
PO Box 937, Great Wilbraham, Cambridge CB21 5JX United Kingdom

All rights reserved
© Ken N. Kamoche, 2007

The right of Ken N. Kamoche to be identified as the
author of this work has been asserted by him in accordance
with Section 77 of the Copyright, Designs and Patents Act 1988.

This book is in copyright. Subject to statutory exception
and to provisions of relevant collective licensing agreements,
no reproduction of any part may take place without the written
permission of Salt Publishing.

Salt Publishing 2007

Printed and bound in the United States of America by Lightning Source
Typeset in Swift 9.5 / 13

*This book is sold subject to the conditions that it shall not,
by way of trade or otherwise, be lent, re-sold, hired out,
or otherwise circulated without the publisher's prior consent
in any form of binding or cover other than that in which
it is published and without a similar condition including this
condition being imposed on the subsequent purchaser.*

ISBN 978 1 84471 320 2 paperback

Salt Publishing Ltd gratefully acknowledges
the financial assistance of Arts Council England

1 3 5 7 9 8 6 4 2

For little emperor James and his mimmie

Contents

The Smell of Fresh Grass   1

Private Lessons   13

The Dream Went Out   24

London Slaves   38

A Glimpse of Life   45

The Warrior's Last Job   56

Random Check   68

Black Fishnet Stockings   83

For a Favourite Niece   94

The Lion's Tears   103

And then the End   114

Acknowledgements   121

The Smell of Fresh Grass

Auntie is steaming *ha gau* dumplings for a late breakfast. The smell of prawns and vinegar fills the air. I stand in the doorway and watch her pour herself a bowl of congee. She scowls at me and asks what I want.

'Where's Ah-Pah?' I ask.

'How the hell should I know?'

I hate her when she's like this. Trouble is, she's always like this. I try to reason with her, the way Ah-Mah used to haggle over prices in Kowloon wet markets. She's not interested. Her face darkens. Her lips are razor sharp. This must be how sharks look when about to strike. I have to speak to Ah-Pah today. Maybe if he's by himself he'll talk to me. I've made my mind up. I'm returning to Hong Kong. I should never have come to Denmark.

'He must have told you where he was going?'

She takes the *ha gau* out of the wok and places them on the Ikea dining table. Then starts to unwrap a *char siu bau* that's bigger than a tennis ball and sets it on the wok. She replaces the lid and glares at me, hands akimbo. God, I hope I never have to see this noodle shop again.

'And even if he did, why should I tell you, Lisa?'

'It's important, auntie.'

She stares at me as if I'm an irritant wasp buzzing around her face but lacking the guts to sting. Then she explodes into laughter, head thrown back and mouth open wide enough to take a whole *char siu bau*. Her laughter reminds me of horses

1

neighing at the Happy Valley racecourse as jockeys ready them for a race. I pick up a laminated menu and twiddle it round like a scorecard. I bite my lower lip, restraining my horse.

'You think he cares about you? He wishes you never came to Copenhagen!'

My head spinning, I hurl the menu at her. It ends up in her congee. She stamps her foot on the floor and glares at me above the rectangular glasses that make her resemble a witch in a horror movie. Her lips curl downwards in the scowl that always follows her laughter.

'I don't believe you!'

'Ho, ho! And why you think he sold your flat, eh? So stupid, la!'

'Just tell me where I can find him, and I promise I won't bother you again.'

She sits down and starts to eat her dumplings, her back to me. I'm standing at the door staring at this little mean woman who ensnared my father and brought him all the way from Hong Kong into this dull, cold country. What did he ever see in her? Was he so desperate after Ah-Mah left him that he was ready to settle for anything? Did he fall for her lies that she was a rich businesswoman?

'Get out of here, Lisa!' she yells. 'You'll find your father killing himself in Christiania!'

'Where is Christiania?'

'How the devil should I know?'

I know she's lying. She has lived in this city for decades. She takes the *char siu bau* out of the wok and starts to poke into it with chopsticks. This must be how she tortures Ah-Pah in his sleep, poking him in the ribs with her red nails. Why do I have to call her auntie, anyway? Just because she sleeps with my father, she thinks she's my replacement mother and can order me about!

'Should never have come here,' she seems to read my mind. 'You don't belong here, Lisa. You'll never make it. You can't even do anything useful in the shop.' She wants me to be her slave. Washing dishes. Cutting the meat up. Defrosting dumplings. She's right. That's not for me.

'Don't worry, I won't be here much longer.' She might as well know now.

Her laughter follows me down the cobbled pavement. If only Ah-Chen were here.

I get off the metro at Christianshavns and peer at the street names. Danish names are so difficult to read. Torvegade. Dronningensgade. Lille Sondervoldstraede. I need to ask someone the way. I hate doing that. Makes them think you're a clueless tourist.

'Excuse me? Where is Christiania?'

'Down Badsmandstraede, to the bottom. Then left.'

'Thank you!' I start to cross the road.

'Be careful! Could be illegal.'

I find it difficult to understand the Danes sometimes, especially their jokes. Did he say *bad men's street*? Illegal? I take measured steps, and long, deep breaths. I stop before I get to the end of the road. All I see is water ahead of me. Part of the canal, or the sea. I have no idea. I stand there like a fool, trying to figure out which way to go.

'You lost?' The voice makes me start. I turn round and see a black man grinning down at me.

'I think I know where you going, love.' His voice is too soft for such a big person. He's over six foot tall, huge muscles sticking out on his arms. A chest as broad as a tree trunk looks ready to burst out of the skimpy t-shirt. Foot-length dreadlocks fall like a mop across his shoulders.

'Je peux vous aider, mademoiselle?'

He sees the perplexed look on my face and laughs.

'I'm sorry, I guess I'm lost.'

'No problem, mademoiselle. Toumane, that's my name. Hi.'

'Hi, I'm Lisa.'

He says he's from Mali. I've never heard of it.

'Is it near South Africa?'

He bursts out into head-thrown-back laughter, just like auntie, but without the rough edge.

'Ah! Ah! Naw, naw, my dear! Miles away, so far away. You see darlin', Africa is so big. Mali is in West Africa. And where you from?'

'Hong Kong,' I whisper, and my face turns hot with embarrassment. He probably thinks I'm ashamed to come from such a tiny place, compared to his Africa.

'Come with me, Lisa' he says, 'I know where you're going.

Everybody round here looking for Christiania. It's the place to be.'

I follow him like a child, as if I'm under a spell. How could he possibly know where I'm going? Some African juju thing?

'Right here, love.'

It looks like a market, music blaring from little wooden shops run by black people with dreadlocks and long-haired Danes in over-sized jackets and surplus army boots.

'Reggae music, man,' says Toumane. It's new to me.

The shops are more like ramshackle kiosks. Their wares are displayed prominently on a sloping counter. I ask Toumane what's that strange greenish-brown substance.

'Grass, man.'

'Grass?'

'What do you call it in Hong Kong?'

The smell hits me. I begin to recognize the burnt-leaves smell at the karaoke in Yau Ma Tei, where I used to work. *Ah ha! Illegal!* I can't believe they're selling and smoking it so openly here. I thought that only happened in Amsterdam. We walk around the market. There are open-air pubs everywhere, full of people puffing away and knocking back pints of Carls Special and Tuborg.

Toumane has appointed himself my tour guide, talking incessantly about the market, which he says is actually a city within a city, teaching me the correct pronunciation of the wares on display, the names of the reggae songs blaring from each kiosk.

'Tourist or customer, Lisa?' he asks. I shake my head.

'You?'

'Moi?' He laughs and points at his chest, which makes me laugh. In Hong Kong people point at their nose.

'Depends. When I have good music, drink strong beer, voila! A joint is not too bad, ma cherie. Pas mal du tout.'

'Actually I'm looking for my father.'

'He's tourist?'

I shake my head. No, maybe a sort of reluctant tourist. What would he be doing here? That woman of his is playing tricks on me. Who does she think she is, stopping me from talking to my own father? *Your father is too tired now, let him rest. His back is in pain.* I know, that's why he's always asking me to walk on his

4

back. But it doesn't do any good. He needs a good massage in Hong Kong, or across the border in ShenZhen where it's much cheaper. He just sits there all day, hunched in the rocking chair, lost in thought. You'd think he was deaf and dumb. Is he dreaming about Ah-Mah? Why can't he just forget her? She broke his heart for God's sake.

I spot him. When did he take up smoking? But, that smell, that thick smoke? It can't be Ah-Pah. He's sitting straight-backed. That's not possible. He seems to be smiling, nodding to that music with loud hypnotic rhythms.

Got to have kaya now
For the rain is falll-iiing.

'Bob, man, the best.' Toumane punches the air the way tennis players do when they score a point. I've no idea who's Bob.

'Bob Marley, man. *Got to have kaya now, for the rain is falll-iiing.*'

It must be about thirty degrees today, and there's not a cloud in the sky.

I've never seen Ah-Pah this relaxed. He seems to be wrapped up in a fantasy. Will he recognize me? I turn to my tour guide. 'My father, I . . .'

'I'll wait for you.'

Ah-Pah is puffing away like those rowdy customers at the karaoke. My heart sinks. Did auntie put him up to this?

'Ah-Pah?'

He looks up and runs a hand through the few strands of graying hair that still cling onto the spotted scalp. He doesn't seem surprised to see me, as though he has been expecting me. Then I realize he doesn't recognize me. I sit beside him, fanning the smoke away with my hand.

'Your back. It seems . . . okay?'

He sucks his lips, staring into space. I might as well not be here. I can't remember a time when he really talked to me. Not a single gentle word. Only criticisms and accusations. And recently there hasn't even been any of that. Just a dead silence between us. Maybe I should buy a joint and smoke my troubles away.

I used to think he was the stranger. He and his woman. But it seems I'm the stranger now. They fit in better than me in this city. They have their noodle shop. They have each other. And they don't need me. Now that they have my money.

'Smoking this . . . helps?'

'In this place, no bad back.'

Bad men's street. But no bad back. So that's alright, then? My stomach muscles tighten. I don't know if it's anger or the smell of this horrible grass. I'm afraid I'm going to throw up.

'Ah-Pah, I'm going away.'

He doesn't respond.

'I'm leaving.'

'Oh, see you later.'

'I'm going back to Hong Kong.'

He inhales deeply and shuts his eyes, as if he's trying to shut me out. There's no need for that. He shut me out of his life a long time ago.

'To do what! Hong Kong is finished! Economy's terrible. This return to China is no good. No good.' He frowns. Like auntie. I can see why they put up with each other. They've become one and the same.

'There's nothing for me to do here.'

'Many things to do, but you're too useless! No brains. Not like your brother.'

I've heard this before. More often than I care to remember. But I've never been able to understand why he thinks Ah-Tim is smarter than me. I don't like discussing Ah-Tim with him. But something tells me it's time to get this off my chest. Now that I'm going. And won't be seeing him again.

'Ah-Pah, what exactly does Ah-Tim do for a living?'

He stares at me as if I've asked him who he is. He clears his throat and spits into the bushes behind us.

'Businessman, what do you think!'

'What kind of business, Ah-Pah?'

He dismisses my question with a downward wave of the hand, as if he's swatting a mosquito.

'If he's such a smart businessman, why is he always borrowing money from me? And he never pays back.'

'Ah-Tim borrows money from you, huh! What money do you have?'

'For years, ever since he finished middle school.'

'Nonsense!'

'Of course he wouldn't tell you. Just like he wouldn't tell you how he makes his money. Smuggling cigarettes. Illegal betting. Horses. Drugs. Football. Illegal car parks. Gambles it all away in Macau. And then comes begging. *Oh Lisa, my big sister, please, you can't neglect me. Just a few big ones before Friday.* I've had enough of him. Your precious businessman son!'

He stares at me with such venom in his eyes I can almost physically feel his hatred. I move to the end of the bench.

'Lying! That's not Ah-Tim!' He goes into a coughing fit.

'It's the truth, Ah-Pah. Ask him what happened to his best friend, Ah-Man. You remember him don't you? Our neighbour in Kowloon City. Same triad. Ah-Man was arrested. He's in Pik Uk now. Two years already. Ah-Tim was very lucky, he was in Macau gambling when the police found all that counterfeit money. Ask Ah-Tim where's Ah-Man. Ah-Man covered for him. Otherwise he too would be in prison now.'

His face is all puffed up and about to explode, like in the cartoons. There, I've just blown away his old-age pension.

'Just jealous!' he spits the words out the way he spits out fish bones, the head bent close to the table so that his chin seems to be jabbing into his chest.

'Jealous? You think I want to be a criminal?'

'He's my son. He's a man! You're just . . . just . . .'

'Just what, Ah-Pah? Just a girl?'

Even now, he still can't utter the words that have troubled him all my life, from the day he walked into the hospital and the nurses said, 'you have a beautiful baby daughter!' He took one look at me and slumped into a seat, as if someone had just died. Ah-Mah always cried when she told me that story.

His chin is now nestled in his chest. He's breathing too fast. Like a man who has just completed a marathon. This is not good. He has a bad heart.

'You've always known he's a useless shit, haven't you? That's why you forced me to sell my flat and give him the money. *Lisa, no need keep flat in Hong Kong. Property market collapsed. Sell. Invest in noodle shop! Help Ah-Tim with his business.*'

I get up before he can respond. My heart is on fire. That flat was the only thing I had. A gift from my Ah-Chen. He called it our little love nest. So many dreams beckoned ahead of us! It was easy to forget he would never leave his wife. I only agreed to the sale to give Ah-Pah face, so he wouldn't be too dependent on that woman. But I don't even think his name is on the deed of that stupid noodle place.

A man walks up to me, with a big smile on his face. I ignore him and walk on. Then I hear him call my name. I stop and face him.

'I'm so sorry, I . . .'

'No problem, Lisa. I see you have things to handle.'

He cannot understand what I'm going through right now. He walks me back to the metro. He seems to have little to do. I ask him what he does for a living.

'Musician, Lisa. I'm a musician.' He gives me a card. 'Chez Afrika, the club where I play. Please come and see us some time. Best African music in Copenhagen. I promise!'

Ah-Pah and auntie are doing their best to ignore me. Auntie is not even yelling at me any more. She seems to have found a new happiness, which she's trying hard to hide, now that she knows I'll be leaving. She got at least half the money. Most of it went to pay the loan sharks who've kept her in business. But they've nearly ruined her with the interest charges. Some of the money helped her diversify. She started to offer *yuhk si chau mihn*, deep fried noodles with shredded pork, and *chau fahn*. Fried rice. *Chau fahn* becomes The Special. A real local favourite down Lisvaeksgade.

I have a reservation to fly in two weeks' time. Can't get a job here. And auntie expects me to slave for her, even while she refuses to make me a partner. One evening as I walk in I find them arguing. They have no shame. There's a customer waiting for her take away *chau fahn*. They go quiet when they see me. They're talking about Ah-Tim. I ignore them and head upstairs. But I can still hear angry voices. I can't stand it. I grab my purse and walk out.

That's when I remember the musician guy. I search in my purse for his card. It's a ten-minute walk. The sun is still shining at nine. That's the one thing I like about this country. It gets dark very late in the summer. But the shops are closed and all you see are people milling around, going to restaurants and pubs. They drink an awful lot in this country, it seems. Hardly surprising, it's the home of Carlsberg.

The streets are filled with girls in mini-skirts and high heels. Men in shorts and t-shirts. They're drunk, or looking forward to getting drunk. Wide grins plastered across their faces. It's like a carnival, people wearing their smiles like masks. You don't know who is beneath the mask. Not that it matters. It's just like being back in Lan Kwai Fong.

The African club is in a narrow street, tucked away between pubs and restaurants. I walk through the door and find an empty table. The place is only half full. The music reminds me of that reggae at Christiania.

I'm still wearing my dark sunglasses and a cap. Toumane doesn't recognize me. He's playing something that looks like a banjo, or a guitar. I've never seen anything like it before. I order a glass of white wine and listen to the music for twenty minutes. It has strong rhythms, and the singing sounds haunting. If I stay here long enough I could get hypnotized. During the break, I take off my sunglasses. Toumane sees me. I'm impressed he remembers my name. He says he's been waiting for me every night for two weeks.

I sit through another set. They finish at 10.30 tonight. Another band will take over at eleven. I want a change of scene. So we find another pub down the road. Toumane tells me stories of African village life and music, and the names of the instruments his band play. The kora, djembe, ngoni, the balafon.

He talks excitedly about traditional Malian music and the soulful Bambara elegies. He's like a teacher explaining things to a child. How the roots of the 21-string kora go back to the reign of the 13th century King Sunjata Keita. When he explains how his band infuses Sengalese mbalax and Zairean soukous with Cuban flute-and-violin charanga vibes and Chicago blues, I give up. I smile, quietly sip my white wine and follow the hand gestures, since the words don't make much sense. For about two hours, I forget the troubles with Auntie, the aloofness of Ah-Pah, and even the receding memories of Ah-Chen.

Toumane seems so organized. Although his family are in Africa he calls them all the time. They're close, and he has his music. Out here so far away, his music is all he has. He doesn't even have a girlfriend. He says he has no time for romance.

'I want to succeed, Lisa. I don't want to play in clubs all my life,' he tells me. 'There's no money in it. Pays the bills, but is that all in life, paying bills? Not enough for me. Pas du tout!'

'What do you want?'

'Sign up with a label and sell CDs! I want the whole world to hear my music. Playing nightclubs is not enough. Not enough!' His eyes are like flashlights.

Tonight I'm in the mood to talk. I don't know why. Maybe it's because I'm leaving. Nothing will matter when I'm gone. I haven't had a single friend the whole time I've been in this city. And now, listening to this musician talk about his dreams exposes the emptiness of my life. Or has it always been like this? Things were good before. Everything changed when that bastard was shot in Mongkok and they all suspected Ah-Chen. Just because they had an argument the night before.

I'll send word, Lisa. I'll send for you. That's what he said before he climbed into the boat in the murky waters of Tai Pang Wan and sailed off to mainland China. *I need to lie low until this thing blows over.* It never did. Three years now, he's been gone. And my life just went down the drain. I lost the love of my life. Then I lost my flat. And now I'm losing my father. And my mind, unless I can get away from here.

Toumane is staring intently into my face. I've no idea how long I've been talking for. But somehow it feels good. I find a packet of tissues and dry my eyes. I haven't had this much to drink since the karaoke days. I don't know if I can find my way home.

'So sad, Lisa, so sad,' says Toumane, over and over again, like a mantra to bring me back to life. There can be no salvation for me now. Even Toumane can see that, and he's a stranger, from a land far away. He smiles, and the smile seems to be coming from somewhere deep in his head, seeping through the skin. So unlike those masks out on the street.

'Are you okay?' I ask him.

'In Africa when the rains come and quench the earth after the oppressive hot season, and the earth swells with pride like a well-fed lion, that's how I feel, Lisa. Then the grass grows everywhere, green, bright and confident. It defies our heavy feet and grows in the footpath. The smell of fresh grass, oh, Lisa, you bring that feeling to me.'

'Your music will always be with you.' I know I'll never see him again. And I know it's time for me to leave. He walks me out and hails a taxi, then takes my hand and kisses it, like in old European movies. My head is spinning. A friend at last. But why now, just when I'm leaving town?

'Call me, Lisa, non?' The taxi pulls away before I can say good-bye.

When I get to the shop, it's almost one o'clock. Auntie is locking up.

'What is this!' she mutters under her breath. I'm about to yell something appropriately filthy when I trip over a carton of noodles and go crashing to the floor. The world darkens and closes in on me. And all I can hear is auntie's laughter, bouncing against the walls of her shop like the sound of pots and pans smashing to the ground.

I wake up late in the morning. It's already 11. I don't know how I ended up in bed. There's a bandage across my forehead. I must have hurt myself real bad. I hear some activity in the shop. Probably auntie making her usual late breakfast. Half an hour later there's a knock on my door. I pretend to be asleep. They've never come to my room before. The door creaks open, and the smell of steamed shrimp dumplings fills the air. I keep my eyes shut. If auntie thinks she can poison me she's very mistaken. I'm not touching her stupid dumplings.

'Lisa, ah?' I open one eye first. With my hangover and the sun shining through the drapes, it's too painful to open both.

Ah-Pah is sitting on the edge of my bed, holding a tray. He still remembers how I liked my breakfast. A few dumplings. A boiled egg, and hot lemon tea. I sit up and study his bowed head. He has lost more hair in recent weeks. I take the tray and thank him. He nods but doesn't say a word. He turns to face the window. I eat my breakfast in silence, not once taking my eyes off him. When I finish I try to place the tray on the floor but he quickly takes it from my hand. In that one instant we make eye contact. The first time in weeks, possibly years. He swallows hard. His Adam's Apple seems to do a summersault.

'Ah-Pah, that's the best breakfast I've had in months.'

His face breaks into a grin. But he's still not looking at me. He reaches into his pocket and hands me an envelope. When I tear it open he's already out of the room.

Two tickets fall out. One-way to Hong Kong.

One in my name. One in his.

We leave the day after tomorrow.

Private Lessons

Today's my last day here. I'm done banging my head against the glass ceiling. They think I don't know why they really hired me. They're talking to dad behind my back. Begging for favours. Work permit renewals. Licenses. Tax and duty waivers. Contracts and tenders. To them the MBA from UCLA was little more than a sanitary towel to absorb all this deception.

It's my turn to join dad's business empire. Mum's right. The family's got to stay together. You can't trust outsiders. Mum's been on my case for two years now. But I felt I needed to prove myself. My brothers won't patronize me any more. *What do these multinationals give you, sis? Big title?* I can't stand Tarus, with that stupid sing-song voice of his. Who cares for a big title? He has no idea what it means to prove yourself out there. Putting your MBA to the test. He joined dad's hotel business straight out of college, on mum's urging, like he didn't have a mind of his own.

Mum seems to think the world outside dad's business is a jungle. They'll hurt you, the people out there, she says. They're jealous of us. You hear what they say about daddy? Don't waste your time fighting the bureaucracy in someone else's firm when you can start at the top. Mum never stops reminding me how they struggled and suffered in the sixties when dad was just starting out. Selling vegetables in the market, the sun beating down on her head like a common peasant. Now she thinks I'm some sort of corporate peasant.

It's a quarter past noon. I'm running late for my lunch appointment with Chuka. I could be wrong, but yesterday she seemed to imply she has new information about her father's disappearance. I don't know why she thinks I can help. The best I can do is console her, and maybe ask around. Someone may have heard something. But what could it be?

Her father is one of those opposition politicians who have become a pain in the government's arse. All they do is call press conferences and hold demonstrations on the streets of Nairobi, accusing the government of all manner of atrocities. They think it will earn them votes. But they're just like a naughty child slapping its mother's calves. One mere wave of the hand and they'll go sprawling on the floor. Breaking their bones. They don't understand the President. He's been patient so far. When he flexes his muscles they'll squeal like rats.

A week ago, before his disappearance, Matega issued a press statement claiming someone was out to 'finish' him. That's how they tap into public sympathy. But when you go around accusing leaders of being corrupt, you can expect someone will be very upset. Rumours are already flying. He has been detained without trial; he has been murdered by some rival; he has fled to a neighbouring country; he's taking cover at some embassy. They give Kenya a bad name, these so-called democrats.

For Chuka's sake I hope they find him. How she's changed since we came back from LA! Boring scholarship law student who had no idea how to party now courts trouble like it's some sort of game.

I ease the car out of the reserved parking and into Loita Street which is already clogging up with the lunch-time traffic.

That's when I see the demonstration. Hundreds, maybe thousands, shouting and waving banners. I'd heard about a planned rally. But wasn't it supposed to be in Uhuru Park? You never know with these democrats. How do they expect to lead the country with this kind of confusion? The noise seems to have engulfed the entire city. Kenyans used to be a humble and peaceful lot. Now the whole country has gone mad. Even illiterate villagers and street sweepers have become political pundits, calling for democracy.

What will they do with it?

I drive into Koinange Street only to find the crowds even more dense there. The whole place is crawling with young men chanting empty slogans for hire. Dressed in old t-shirts and second-hand jeans. Drenched in sweat. They've brought the traffic to a standstill. I turn up the music on the stereo to drown the noise. After fifteen minutes I manage to reach Kenyatta Avenue. At this rate I doubt I'll ever make it to Westlands on time. I hate to keep Chuka waiting. She'll be teasing me about lack of professionalism blah blah blah. I'm anxious to see if she's alright. She and her dad are very close. I hate to imagine what his disappearance is doing to her.

The demonstrators are clambering up the stationary vehicles, forcing people to get out of their cars and chant *Power to the people!* Do they really think people want this democracy crap shoved down their throats?

I sit still not daring to move, and watch them out of the corner of my eye, marching, chanting. Waving clenched fists in the air, pulling motorists out of their cars and making them yell *Power! Democracy!* These young men are like hyenas baying for blood.

Up ahead there's a commotion. They have forced a man up on the bonnet of his BMW, searching his car, for God-knows what. The poor victim looks familiar. A prominent businessman. They say they want democracy, but this is beginning to look like a communist revolution. Some are howling *Release Matega!* Brandishing placards with pictures of Chuka's father. Someone is probably emptying the businessman's pockets. Why are the police taking so long to come and break this up?

I have to get out of here. I don't care about the car. I manage to hold the door open against the tide of protestors and squeeze my way out. Ten people shouting war-cries and democracy slogans surround me. Their blood-shot eyes and the breath reeking from their mouths betray an over-indulgence in illicit *chang'aa.* I try in vain to snake my way through the wall of protestors. Two of them jump on top of my car and start chanting *Power to the people!* Like some sort of mantra. If they get the power they're calling for this country is finished. We're all dead. Now I can see my sister's wisdom in leaving for Paris to pursue her passion for fashion design. God, I shouldn't have to put up with this. I should never have left George. We would have been happy now, raising a family in Santa Monica and spending lazy afternoons on the beach. The sand on the beach is so hot in the summer it forces you to stay in the water and swim. And stay in shape.

They drag me out of my reminiscing, like in a nightmare, and straight on to the bonnet of my car. As I struggle to free myself, my jacket comes apart down my back and I can feel it hanging down my shoulders like two edges of a scarf.

Repeat: Power to the people!

Say: Release Matega!

'I can't. I'm not in the opposition. Let me go.'

'Just say power to the people and you can leave,' one of them growls. I look into his eyes. He's probably a first-year university student, only here because of his friends. By himself he probably doesn't even have the guts to approach a woman.

'What if I don't?' I lock eyes with him. The crowd is unrelenting, banging on the car and charging the air up with howls and whistles.

The boy averts his eyes, relaxes his grip on my shoulder and glances furtively at the crowd. Over his shoulders I see the TV cameras trained on us. I shake off the boy's grip and try to push him off my car. But before I can get away from the other man's grip, three other people climb up on the car and threaten to strip me naked unless I obey. It's getting too crowded on my two-seater Mercedes.

'Mama, please do it. You know we mean business.' The man is leaning towards me, speaking in a low voice. A gust of *chang'aa* breath hits my face, and my knees begin to give. There's no way out. I gaze straight into the cameras and scream:

'Power to the people!'

Hoi-yehhh! Hehhh! Power to the people! A tremor runs down my spine.

'One more time, mama, for the people. For justice.'

'Power to the people!'

Hoi-yehhh! Hehhh! Power!

Free Matega!

Freedom for the people!

Down with the government!

'Can I go now?' I'm out of breath, sweating and reeling with an intoxicating sense of excitement.

As I climb down the car, glancing about me like a sheep surrounded by hyenas, someone grabs my handbag and empties the contents on the boot. I scramble for my things, screaming above the commotion. I manage to snatch back my wallet. They'll have to fight me for it. For a split second my wallet hangs in the air, as if trying to decide whether to drop or fly away. A tall, skinny fellow with unkempt hair grabs it and starts to search inside. I can't reach his face with my outstretched nails as two people hold me back. His bloodshot eyes look like dying embers, his face gleaming with sweat. He pulls my ID card out and reads my name.

'Kabang! This is the daughter of the corrupt minister!'

He doesn't know he's on camera. He'll pay for this. He throws my wallet over his shoulder, like a spent cigarette butt. My cries for help are drowned by *Power to the people! Free Matega!* chants. Held in a vice-like grip on all sides, I watch as someone pulls my shoes off and throws them into the crowd, in different directions. They might as well kill me now.

Let the feet of the thieving rich feel the angry heat of the starving earth!

They are kicking my car, and smashing it up with whatever they can lay their hands on, dustbins abandoned on the pavement, broken street signs. Everyone dashes away just as soon as an angrier section of the crowd deflates the wheels and sets my car on fire.

All around, people are abandoning their cars and fleeing from the impending explosion. I'm running barefoot on the rubbish-drenched road, choking from the stifling mix of sweat and the smoke from my smoldering car. The flames rise to the sky, and when the explosion comes I'm already running up Waiyaki Way, trying to flag down a taxi.

Unable to get a taxi on the road, I make my way towards the Serena Hotel. In the sweltering heat I take off the torn jacket and let it fall on the pavement. A man in old dirty clothes picks it up and melts into the crowd.

The eyes of the drivers at the taxi rank at the hotel are filled with a mixture of pity and disgust, as though they were looking at a mad woman walking nude in the street. The first driver I approach simply looks away, a cigarette dangling on his lips. I stand there for a moment, wanting to strangle him. For his insolence he could lose his license. And car. I'm afraid my feet are covered in blisters. I wrench open the door of the second taxi and jump in the back. The driver is already waving me away. I hold a finger close to his face and, in my best American accent, demand to be taken to Karen Estate.

His jaw drops to his chest, his eyes like those of a mouse cornered by a cat in a cul-de-sac.

'Step on it, man, will ya?' I just want to see those eyes again.

He speeds off like a most-wanted escaping from the police.

Mum nearly has a fit when she sees the state I'm in. How can I answer her questions? I just want to go to my old room and forget all this madness. What is this country coming to? Mum leads me to the living room. Dad's home for lunch, with two friends. One of them is the Indian billionaire, Chopra. Their eyes are glued to the TV which is now broadcasting the mayhem in the city, cars on fire, rioters looting shops, police trying to disperse them with teargas. The camera replays an earlier scene with a group of people standing on a car.

Among the demonstrators calling for democracy was the daughter of a prominent minister. Unfortunately we were unable to interview her and she was observed escaping from the scene of a burning car. Eye-witnesses confirmed that this was the event which sparked off the riot and marred an otherwise peaceful demonstration. The police want to interview her.

And there I am, shouting like a student activist: 'Power to the people!' I cover my ears and bury my face in my lap. The living room fills with gasps of horror. I steal a glance at dad, who is as still as a statue, rendered mute by anger and disbelief. My mother puts her arms around me and bursts into tears.

'Poonie . . . why? What came over you . . .?'

'Dad . . . it's not like that . . .' I look away. Little Angel just became Little Devil.

'Just tell me why, darling. Don't worry about the police. It's nothing. Nothing to worry about. But, you joining these . . . these democracy people!' He spits the words out as if he's afraid he'll choke on them. My head is buried in mum's shoulder.

We now take you directly to the Matega family for the latest on the disappearance of this popular opposition leader. A man who has stood steadfast against the culture of corruption and political ineptitude. The man whose mysterious disappearance a week ago has shocked the nation and galvanized the pro-democracy campaign.

The camera pans to Chuka. I hope she'll forgive me for standing her up. She's wearing her usual multi-coloured traditional kitenge and matching headscarf. But the warmth of her colours does not reach her face, the mask of mourning. She is flanked by two of those so-called human rights lawyers.

We have evidence that my father was threatened. He received a phone call from a powerful government official, after which he was reduced to a man afraid of his own shadow because he sensed he was looking death in the face. We want to talk to this strongman. We believe this information will lead us to my father's whereabouts.

A hush falls upon the room.

Are you prepared to name the minister who threatened your father?

We only want to ask the minister what he said to my father.

What is the name of the minister?

Mister Rupert Kabang!

A collective gasp reverberates through the room. Mum is wailing as though there has been a death in the family. Dad is like a raging bull. Smashing his beloved Ming Dynasty vases. Kicking the dog out of the room. I start to amble out. Chopra is up on his feet, blocking my way.

'What are you knowing about this, miss?' he demands. Our eyes lock like bulls' horns.

'Jesus Christ, Chopra!' My father looks ready to bite his head off. 'What!'

'Rupert, I'm understanding she was in demonstration, c'rrect? You saw just now on television, no?'

'Haah-iyah, what? Just . . . just . . . sit down, right?'

I peer into my father's eyes. The gentle eyes that caressed his Little Angel and made her glow with pride and admiration now resemble red-hot coals. He was always a step away from God himself. But now I'm looking into the heart of the same fury and hostility that threatened my life on the street. Covering my ears, I trudge to my old room.

When I wake from the torment of afternoon nightmares, it's

already five. The house is abuzz with guests. It's like a war council in session. I count at least fifteen limousines in the drive. I recognize many of them. Lawyers and politicians. I'm in no mood for any more of this. I'll borrow one of mum's cars and go home to my apartment. I need something inconspicuous, like the VW Golf.

But something tells me to stay a little longer. I take the north exit and wander round the house, past the swimming pool and flower gardens. When I was a teenager I loved to sit under the window of dad's study. That's where he holds important private meetings. I would sit there for hours, listening to their conversations about politics and business. I called it my private lessons.

That's where I learned what an important person dad was in the country, and the extent of our wealth. That's where I learned how important it is to make money, and to acquire power to protect it. As my father used to say, the crocodile learns to whip foes away with its tail, yet allows the plover into its mouth to pick its teeth after a meal. I learned more in the private lessons than in lecture theatres at UCLA.

I'm ready for a new lesson. But the voices are muffled. All I hear is Chuka's mournful voice on the phone. *You can help me, Poonie. Just ask around, and be careful. Can you imagine how I feel, with father missing?* No, I could not. She was struggling not to break down. She's always been the toughest amongst my friends. I'll never forget the day the cops busted a college party and found coke and joints and wanted to arrest us all. We would have been deported. It was the first time in my life I knew dad's protective hand couldn't reach his Little Angel. When I called Chuka she knew exactly what to do, like she was reading from a textbook.

But the voice that spat out my father's name on television this afternoon is still ringing in my ears. I have to convince Chuka she's barking up the wrong tree. It's just not possible. My father is the most gentle, the kindest, the most loving father one could ever wish for, and one of the most illustrious politicians in this country. None of that grime they've been throwing at him has ever stuck. And he has always forgiven them.

'What are you doing here, Poonie?' Mum's voice startles me. She's picking flowers for the dining table.

'Shhh!' I beckon her to sit beside me on the grass, where we can bask in the luscious smells of the roses and bougainvillea, and watch the calm surface of the swimming pool, responding with gentle ripples to the evening breeze.

Eyes wide open, mum takes tentative steps and sits down, then buries her nose in the fragrance of the roses.

'Mum, why do you wear these old-fashioned clothes?'

Mum still dresses like the rural housewife in her 1960s hazy black and white pictures.

'They suit me, Poonie, don't you see?'

'Mum, this is 1997!'

'Years are just numbers, my dear. Look at this rose. Isn't it pretty?'

They've found what? Father's voice thunders through the open window.

It seems there were no crocodiles in the lake, Rupert.

I can't believe this! Haah-iyah, what!

Me too, Rupert, I'm not believing this. Ridiculous, no?

Relax, Rupert. We'll take care of it. We always do, right? There's no proof. The stupid guys should at least have tied rocks to it.

This is surely the end . . .that phone call. Jesus! Haah-iyah!

Is okay, I'm thinking. We're having everything, c'rrect? Judges. Police, no?

Sure thing. We'll clean it up. If nothing else, we'll keep them in court forever.

Hah! Hah! Hoh! Hoh!

'Where do you think we should put these?'

'What!' I curse myself for hissing at mum.

'The roses . . .'

'Mum, did you . . . did you hear that?'

'Your daddy has many enemies, working hard for this country. And for us, dear.'

My hands acquire a life of their own. Grabbing the roses. Squashing them, oblivious of the thorns. Past lessons wash over my troubled mind, like a revision lesson. *Haah-iyah, he's offering only 10%? Forget it.* I look back now. Over the years. Lessons of a lifetime. *Do these foreigners know who they're dealing with? Fifty percent or nothing!* International trade was like a landmine-infested battlefield. Got a B-plus for that. I remember the professor's comments: excellent use of real-life African examples. *We'll cut them down like trees, Chopra.* Sometimes the lessons were so arcane. *Put a few millions in the party coffers. You'll surely make minister this time, Rupert boy!* Who said business and politics didn't mix? Networking. Strategic alliances. *Chopra, this thing needs cleaning up. It's going to be a big stink if this democrat guy gets his way.*

'You'll hurt yourself, dear. You know tomorrow you have a new job. You have to help your father.'

'It's over, mum . . .' Blood rushes out of my head. I'm going to fall.

'What is it, Poonie?'

'It's no longer private. Not for me.'

'Darling, what are you talking about?'

'This lesson.' I breathe the words out but don't understand what I'm saying.

The perplexed look on mum's face quickly disappears, and she smiles. That calm, patient smile she responds with when dad argues with her or raises his voice.

'Pray for your daddy, like we used to when you were a little girl, and he would pick you up, kiss you and say, oh, my Little Angel. Remember how he bounced you up and down, and you would just swell with pleasure!'

Blinded by tears, I can't see but can only feel mum drying my hands, wiping the petals and blood away. It feels as if she's wiping the memory of Chuka and her daddy off my mind. It's a memory that doesn't belong here. Were the lessons in a language I didn't understand? I was so stupid?

'Mum, you heard . . .'

'Darling, many words have filled my ears. You have no idea. But what is important, it's family, and the things we have. Our name, dear. Our position.'

'But mummy . . .'

'You did the right thing before, darling. The words filled your ears, but you kept in mind our name. Daddy's name.'

My knees buckle. I collapse into mum's arms. 'My friend, Chuka . . .?'

'You'll be a good General Manager. In your new job, dear. For daddy.'

'For da . . . da . . . daddy.'

Mum lifts me to my feet and holds me tight. Her arms feel hard, like the bark of a tree.

'Yes, dear. For daddy. Forget daddy's enemies. Let's pick some fresh roses, yes? For daddy?'

She smiles her long-suffering smile again, and leads me away from the window.

The Dream Went Out

'This is going to be our big break, my brother.' Laughter. 'This is our chance! We'll make it, I tell you. This is the dream that came true!'

Making it was all the rage. Nobody wanted to remain a nobody. They wanted to make it, to move on. But who would dream the dream of genuine freedom, freedom from the daily debilitating struggle of their lives? Karani yearned for that dream. He wanted to break free, and fly like a bird, to a nest well and truly feathered with crisp shilling notes.

Making it big and filling in the void in lives that started with so much promise but usually ended up hanging precariously on the edge of pecuniary solipsism. The great dream that too often took the place of good old-fashioned work. But work did not seem to mean anything any more. It became the empty school room promise that delivered little in the job market.

Just look at Charlie (Chah Lee to friends and non-friends alike). They said. *See how he just recently started from nothing and now as a somebody runs a fleet of matatu minibuses, and a brand new C-class Merc!*

Pretty soon Nairobi won't be big enough for Chah Lee. The dream gets bigger than the dreamer. Yet, little was said about the money that changed hands to lend the dream a semblance of reality. The money that, like a furious April thunderstorm, washed away the myth that it couldn't be done. A few plum plots of land were 'allocated' to deserving citizens for services that were never clearly defined. But no one dared sully Chah Lee's reputation. Or that of some officer in the Lands Office.

So, citizen Chah Lee, he of the imprecise services to an ill-defined community, placed the plots on the market even before the ink had dried on the quickly prepared transfer documents. In no time at all, Chah Lee was the embodiment of the new society of successful entrepreneurs. It was all so effortless. So much easier than they predicted in economics textbooks that made university such a bore for Karani and Olu.

Demand and supply curves. What irrelevant nonsense! Karani had quickly discovered that in modern Kenya, all you needed was a friend or two in the right places. Supply and demand followed. You placed your demand. He supplied. And you supplied a little something in return. And the cycle went on. Just like a dream.

But Karani didn't even know about the new deal in town. The deal Chah Lee was spinning like a spider's web around the city. The world of tablets, pellets and syringes. For Olu, this was the dream that came true. Karani could remember exactly how the decision was made. It was Olu's idea. Much of what he did to make a living was often Olu's idea. Ever since high school. Olu's Nigerian parents worked in Nairobi, or so the story went. Never really clear what they did. Consular connections. Business. Consultancy. Trade. Identities bandied about to lend credence to a story that shifted with the prevailing listener.

Who cared? Olu justified himself in sports. He provided much-needed muscle for the rugby scrum. Handy with the hockey stick, especially when in defence of the school's injured pride. Lashing out at hapless rivals from some upstart school. Defining moments indeed, when Olu shone through as more Kenyan than the Kenyan-born, his accent notwithstanding.

Years later; college in; college out, and Olu styled himself The Broker. A Mister Fix-it of sorts. Equipped with a legitimating Bachelor of Arts. You wanted it done, you talked to Olu. The broker with the winning grin and expansive persuasive gestures as he said, *Just leave it with me.*

For the right price, Olu could fix anything, or so the myth went. But nothing excessively illegal. His style was to make money. Nice and legit; or at least, almost legitimate. That's why he called it legit. Almost there. Between a dream and the reality it sought to enact. Olu the dream giver talked serious money. That was always the plan, anyway. Never mind that serious money and Olu had never crossed paths. But not for want of trying.

'This is going to be different, my brother; take my word for it. It's our big break.'

'How can you be so sure?'

'Piece of cake, my brother. I've got contacts all over Lagos. We'll have the stuff out there and our dues coming in here faster than you can swallow a pellet.'

'Be realistic, Olu!'

'Trust me on this, man. Leave it with me. Am I The Broker or what?'

Karani was a nice guy to pull things off with. He could buy into most plans with a minimum of fuss. He found it easier to place his trust in those who made it all seem so easy. If only making it was as smooth as the talk that preceded it. Making it sound easy was so much easier than actually *making it*.

But even when they didn't deliver, Karani was forgiving enough to allow them another chance to sell him yet another dream. He bought into one dream after another, like the gullible pedestrian forever under the spell of the street con-artist. Dreams drew him closer to the world he feared he was doomed to experience second-hand. A world of riches and power. A world as ethereal as it was intoxicating.

Tossing the coin was the easy part. The mere flip of a coin. Heads you go; tails I go. In through the head; out by the tail-end. A long journey for the stuffed condoms, through the unfortunate body of he who desperately sought the transition from nothing to something. Nobody to somebody. Heads and tails.

Karani did the honours. He took a long hard look at the coin, and saw the President staring up at him as though to remind him *he* was still in charge, in spite of what the opposition activists said. The coin hit the air. Tail chasing head. Head chasing tail. A dance of the macabre embellished by the intermittent flash as the sun rays kissed the receding surfaces of the dancing silver coin. Not a cloud in sight. Only the silver lining ahead of the imminent storm.

It was just his rotten luck. He was going to have to swallow the pellets. His face fell.

Olu tried to hide the sense of relief that swept over him.

'Don't lose heart, my brother. One of us has to do it. Trick is: stay away from food on the trip. And, therefore stay away from the loo. Otherwise you literally flush our future down the toilet. That's where we are now, remember? Down the toilet. And that's where we're trying to GET THE HELL OUT OF!'

Karani glared at him, not sure he needed that sort of pep talk.

'Tell you what. For the extra risk you're taking, an additional 10 per cent in your favour, sir. Honest to God!'

'What do you mean, ten? Thirty, or I'm out. Thirty!'

Olu slapped him playfully on the back. He loved it when Karani occasionally displayed some evidence, no matter how inconsequential, of his capacity for a losing battle. They haggled and argued, eventually settling on sixteen, just below Olu's prior unspoken concession of twenty. Karani silently congratulated himself on what he considered a profitable piece of bargaining.

'This is a sweet sixteen victory, my brother! You're a lucky man. Let's drink to that.'

Yeah! This must have been how Chah Lee felt, when confronted with the intoxicating smell of money. Chah Lee the model entrepreneur. The hero of the dispossessed and desperate to possess.

As the evening wore on and the reality of the deal became clearer, no amount of Tusker could drown Karani's sense of apprehension. Sweet sixteen? He couldn't imagine any sweetness in swallowing condoms stuffed hard with heroin. But he drank the beer anyway. Olu was doing the buying, which was unusual in itself. The broker was almost always broke.

Phone calls were made. Contacts established. Code names created and memorised. The deal was set up. The big one. They were finally going to make it.

'We'll pull this thing off if it's the last thing we do, my brother.'

The words rang in his ears over and over again as he sank onto his bed later that night, too drunk to undress or even throw the blankets over his haggard frame. The little flat in

Kahawa West would soon be too small for his imminent status as a somebody. He had been a nobody for too long. It was time to emerge. Into the world of latter-day entrepreneurs. *Look out Chah Lee, here I come!*

Two weeks later, Karani was in Bangkok. A contact picked him up at Don Muang Airport and drove him to a room on Soi 5, off the supposedly strategic transport artery but forever traffic-clogged Sukhumvit highway. The contact didn't speak much. He didn't even give a name. The game was nameless. As long as it wasn't named, it wasn't happening. And the players retained a mystical anonymity. Would-be somebodies wrapped around the protective shreds of nobodies. Little was said on the half hour drive into town. Karani was in no mood for small talk anyway.

He took note of the bad driving, the Thai characters on billboards hanging from buildings, the posters of beautiful girls advertising everything from cars to skin care products. An accident on the road forced the traffic to a halt. He could see exasperated Thais talking into their mobile phones. Ladies took the opportunity to touch up their make-up. Some ate their breakfast with one hand, the other hand on the wheel. Heavily armed police officers on motorbikes wound their way through the traffic to the scene of the accident, their blue flashing lights surprisingly bright in the early morning misty air.

Eventually the traffic started to move again. Karani could vaguely make out in the distance a motorbike so mangled up he hated to imagine what its passengers might have looked like.

'Motorcy!' muttered the taciturn contact, shaking his head.

'Motorcy?' But of course. Who needs the full name? There wasn't much left of that particular one anyway. Motorcycle that was once something quickly becomes a nothing. Just a motorcy, to the nameless contact. The two lives it carried as good as destroyed as the young taxi-cyclist attempted dangerous manoeuvres to beat the traffic and run a few more trips during the lucrative rush hour.

'Terrible.'

'Motorcy in Klungthep tellible. Too much acciden, you know.'

'Kung what?'

'Klungthep. Thai name for Bangkok.'

The air-conditioned Mercedes hardly prepared him for the gust of humid air that hit him as he stepped onto the *soi*, the lane, and walked into the lobby of a characterless hotel that only passed for a hotel presumably because it took guests in for a few hundred baht. Karani spent the day sleeping off the jet lag. The long flight had taken its toll on one whose prior flying experience was limited to the occasional flight from Nairobi to Mombasa while he worked as an assistant sales manager for a multinational firm before venturing out on his own and then hooking up with Olu The Broker.

The contact with no name gave him a wad of baht, and muttered, 'food . . . cigalette. Aloun here.' Then he gave him a mobile phone and a supply of sim cards. Someone would contact him later that evening.

'Use difflen one ewy time after you get call. Wey importan. Thlow ol one in garbage bin on steet. No in hotel. You get call later. Don't call anyone. Don't call Kenya.'

He nodded. Probably the longest speech mister taciturn contact ever made in his life. It came out like a recorded voicemail message. Alone in the hotel room, he looked out of the window. The traffic stretched out for miles. Tuk-tuks clambered onto the pavements. Motorcys sped at breakneck speed between lanes.

The musical tone of the mobile woke him up. It was already dark. He glanced at his watch. Almost seven. He was instructed to go out and have dinner. *Tomollow no eat!* Another call would come through at 11pm.

'Change sim card now. Use card mark "2".'

'Okay.' *Over and out!* The intrigue was beginning to take on a new character. He smiled to himself. *Sounds good. Alpha to Control. Tomollow no eat. Roger that. Over and out.*

He walked down the street, studying the names on the menus displayed at the doors. *Tom yum gong. Som tam. Thong muan.* The pictures were easier to decipher. Everything was soaked in chilli. Little green and red pieces.

Unsure about all that spicy food, he settled on a Middle-Eastern looking place. The smell of roast meat so reminded him of the Kenyan *nyama choma* delicacy. When he asked what it was, the heavily bearded man told him it was lamb. Not quite his beloved goat *nyama choma*, but close. Afterwards he wandered around the streets and decided to have a drink. The bar was a little deserted. Maybe it was still early. He saw a few girls chatting in the corner.

'You wan Thai beer? Singha beer *dee mahk*.' Very good. The charming waitress smiled sweetly at him. He nodded, remembering posters informing him he was in the Land of Smiles. Miss Smile placed an unfamiliar beer in front of him. He took a sip. It was good; only a little more bitter than the Tusker he was accustomed to. Presently, another big smiler sidled up to him. He couldn't take his eyes off her. He was captivated by the long black hair, smooth brown skin, and the sweet, soft smile that seemed to have been etched permanently on her finely chiselled face.

'*Sawasdee, kha!*'

'Hi there.'

'No speak Thai? You leply, *sawasdee Klap.*'

'Okay. *Sawasdee klap.*'

'*Dee mahk!*'

She clapped her hands like a child who had won a prize.

'Wo you name?

'Karani.'

'Kaani? Nice mee you. Me? Kai. Kai mean chicken. Is nickname. Thai people like funny nickname.'

He laughed, and realised it was the first time he had laughed in weeks.

'Nice to mee you, Kai.' He meant it from the bottom of his tortured heart. It was so nice to forget for a while the challenge of ingesting those damn pellets that were supposed to change his life and Olu's forever.

'Is good luck I mee you.'

'Really?'

'Your name, Kaani. My name, Kai. Almost same-same, no?' He burst out laughing again.

'Weh you fom?'

He told her.

'First time come Thailand?'

'Yeah. Arrived today.'

'You like?'

He nodded.

'You buy me cola?'

He summoned Miss Smiley Barmaid. Kai put her hands together and bowed in a thankful *wai* when the drink arrived. Then she edged closer. He could smell her perfume, and feel the warmth her lithe body exuded as she gently leaned against him. He was being ensnared by a charm he had no will to resist. She placed a soft hand on his lap.

'You wan go with me?'

His heart missed a beat. He couldn't believe this gorgeous thing was offering herself to him. Her hand was now rubbing the inside of his thigh.

'You give me tip, yes? I go with you.'

Oh, so that's the game!

'Life so hard, Kaani. My mother, she fight with my father, always. Them mad, I tell you!' The venom in her eyes and her voice seemed incongruent on the postcard pretty face. 'I leave home las month. Now need pay apartment. So expensive, and I share with two lady.' She gripped his hand tightly as though she needed his protection. He was on his second beer. The bar was filling up. The music got louder. A thoroughly scratched up remix of eighties chart-busters. Grandmaster Flash and the Furious Five. Furiously having a go at the dealer on the street corner.

Miss Smiley Barmaid dimmed the lights. A couple danced languidly on the tiny dance floor.

'I go college. Study design. Now, *mai mee satang*. No money. My flens, them buy Plada, Chanel. Kai, no affor. Wo you wan me do? Kai also like fashion. Plada bag, so pletty. Fendi also nice. You see? Kaani, you need hel me.' She looked so helpless, her hair falling in a protective veil over one eye.

'This tip, ahm. . .,' he glanced quickly over his shoulder. 'Tip, eh, how much, Kai?'

'Up to you,' she whispered, blowing him a kiss. The soft hand snaked itself under his shirt and gently rubbed his chest.

My! She's so forward.

'You stay hotel? Apartment? We go?'

'Let me think about it.'

'Is good chance I mee you today.'

He wondered why.

'Because soon I leave Thailand. My boyfen him ask me mally him. Ewey day him call me as me wen you wan come New Yo? Him falang, you know.' Foreigner.

'So when are you going?'

'Don know. Not sure if him selios. Kai scare go Amelica. Now after 9-11 Amelica them no like foleners. Them scare tellolist. But him good man, my boyfen. Him sen me money. Amelica dollar. I no need work. But sometime cannot affor shopping. Maybe you hel me?'

'I think about it.' *Maybe boyfen hel you.*

He turned his mind to the Singha beer, and drank quietly for a long soul-searching moment. Kai rested her head on his shoulder and left him to his thoughts. Her hand remained under his shirt.

The vibracall of the mobile jolted him out of his reverie.

'Back to hotel. Someone mee you. Fifteen minutes.'

Shit!

He had forgotten the nameless contacts as he sat there basking in the promise of a night of passion with Miss Little Smiley Chicken. Too bad. He leaned close to her to smell her one more time. He wouldn't be able to help with the Prada thing, or was it brown Fendi handbag?

Maybe Mister New Yo falang boyfen would see to it she got a nice Gucci mobile phone holder while he was at it. She didn't seem disappointed he was leaving so soon, and without her. Maybe she was simply good at masking the disappointment beneath the omniscient charming smile.

'Tomollow come bar?'

'Yeah.'

'I wey for you!'

Tomollow no eat! Tomollow come bar!

He unlocked the door and walked into his room and was shocked to see two men sitting there, watching television in the semi-darkness. For a moment he wondered whether he was in the right room. He recognised his jacket on the bed. He knew better than to ask how the strangers got in and what they were doing there. Four Singha beers, but he still remembered the rules of the nameless game. The men were not there. You didn't ask questions. The visit never took place. Over and out!

The uninvited guests wore dark glasses and baseball caps that covered half the face. They did not particularly look like they were prepared for small talk, nor did they bother to introduce themselves.

'Sit down. Enough fun in bar. Time for work now.'

Karani eyed them both carefully, making up his mind this was the last time he was getting involved in this sort of business. He made a mental note to break Olu's neck when he got back to Nairobi.

'Today you need tlaining learn to swallow.'

By this time, Pretty Little Chicken had been relegated to a fantasy that never was. The nameless contact possibly-leader took out a packet from his pocket. Inside there were three hard pellets filled with a whitish substance.

'Just powder.' A curt explanation with a dismissive wave of the hand. 'No ploblem for you. Tomollow it come out. You do again. Need learn, you see. In plane you spend so much hours, how many? Ten? You get use, you see? No food. No water. Nothing. Okay, take one. Swallow. No ploblem.'

'You sure?' He looked carefully at the pellets and a shadow crossed over his face.

'Sure! No ploblem.' The contact patted him on the shoulder reassuringly. 'I know. First time, no easy. But later, you get use. Become expert. You make money!' The two nameless contacts shared a laugh and puffed furiously on their cigarettes.

If he disregarded the somewhat musical accent he could almost hear Olu's voice. The same message. Different voices. Different cities. Same game. A nameless game. A dream in the making. They all made it sound so easy. He selected a pellet as though he were selecting a cigar and promptly threw it into his mouth with an exaggerated flourish. The pellet got stuck in his throat and the contacts had to slap him hard on the back to stop him choking to death. Several attempts later and all the three were safely ensconced within the dark depths of his bowels.

'You see? Is easy, no ploblem. In Thai, we say, *mai mee panhaa*.'

'Oh, really. My me what?'

'*Mai mee panhaa!*'

'I see. *Mai mee panhaa!*'

No ploblem. The contacts rubbed his shoulders, laughing deliriously.

It took a few more days to get it right. Though the contacts declared there was no problem, it wasn't easy, this business of swallowing condoms full of a harmless white powder and waiting for them to work their way through his gut and into the toilet.

The pain shot through him like an angry raging fire. It felt as though someone was trying to wring his insides out of him with the skin still on. The pain came in spasms, reverberating through his whole body and even taking away the power to yelp in agony or cry for help. Spasm after spasm hit him and before he knew it he was hallucinating. Spasms of pain in a macabre dance with the turbulence. Heads and tails. Air pockets. *Please return to your seats and fasten your seatbelts.*

He was vaguely aware of the commotion around him as people tried to help. Before he lost consciousness he visualised the stewardess bending towards him and trying desperately to help him sit up. *Come to me, Kai! Come to me! Is so lucky I mee you!*

But even that kind gesture fizzled away as he slipped into unconsciousness. She was probably the same one who had smiled in muted surprise when he said he didn't want to eat anything.

'*Something to drink, sir?*'

'No. I'm fine. I just want to sleep. Exhausted, you see.' *Today no eat. Tomollow come bar, my Kai.*

He had remembered his lesson well. The nameless contact had been a good instructor. Patient with a touch of kindness, after the initial cold business-like manner. Well, this was a business, after all. Millions were at stake. Amelica dollar. Thai baht. Nigerian naira. Kenyan shillings. The stewardess had kept an eye on him just to be sure. Probably part of her training too. Perhaps her instructors had names. Perhaps their game had a name. Exhausted, you see. But she didn't pay much attention. It wasn't such a long flight, from Dubai to Nairobi.

In any case, would she have been aware he hadn't eaten anything on the much longer flight from Bangkok? Would she have taken note of his discomfiture when the plane hit air pockets and shook for a good ten minutes while the captain's voice came through, talking of turbulence and seatbelts? Maybe she had been alerted. Intelligence. Supposed to be shared. Look out for the passenger who abstains from food and drink. Maybe she didn't think anything of it. Can be tiring, looking after a couple of hundred passengers. A mule can easily slip through the wide lapses of attention. They left it with him.

Nobody stopped him in Dubai where he endured an excruciating three hour transit. Look out for the tell-tale signs. All spelt out in the rule-book. Too many risks, nowadays. Even Smiley Kai on her fashion trail knew of the threat of tellolist.

When he glanced out of the oval-shaped window and saw the fiery clouds as the plane approached Jomo Kenyatta International Airport, he was struggling to contain the turbulence in his own belly. The pellets, packed liked sardines in the middle of his bowels, were starting to respond to the peristaltic motions he remembered from Form Two biology. In those days it was simply bio. Ba-yo. They made it sound like a board game. Fancy a game of ba-yo? Ba-yo teacher wore a low-cut top. When she leaned over the tall lab table, you could see a tantalising cleavage which promised so much to thirteen year-old hormonally-charged boys. But delivered only pubescent fantasy through the clouds of smoke from prohibited cigarettes in overgrown bushes. But this was no game.

And figuring out what those clouds were seemed like a convenient subterfuge to take his mind off the worries about what might or might not happen. Were they cirrus, nimbus, cumulo-nimbus? Heavily bearded geog teacher came to mind as the first spasm struck. And the inscrutable clouds lost their allure. The turbulence out there, thirty thousand feet up just didn't matter any more. He was frothing at the mouth. His feeble frame swayed uncontrollably from side to side. As though he was the only one affected by the turbulence.

Terrified passengers screamed and started to wonder if it was something in the food they had eaten. Was it a new form of terrorist attack? Oh my God! First they crash planes into buildings. Then anthrax letters. Now they're poisoning us!

Cabin crew called for calm. There was no doctor in the cabin. If there was, he or she stayed quiet. The captain radioed for emergency landing rights. An ambulance was waiting. Lights flashing, just like on that misty morning on the road from Don Muang Airport. An accident on the road then. An even nastier accident in the depths of his bowels on the way to another airport. The blue flashing lights in Bangkok and Nairobi remained unchanged, while the lights in his soul were dimming by the minute.

They whisked him away, fitted with oxygen and a drip. But he wouldn't have known anything about this, because he was already in a coma. The pellets responding to the digestive enzymes and peristaltic motions in the gut had struggled to retain their contents. But one of them broke loose, sending the white substance straight into his blood stream. A pellet worth thousands of naira on the streets of Lagos, and thousands more in Nairobi. Now they were all worthless.

Maybe he should have eaten that hot spicy *tom yum gong* soup, with that succulent lemon flavour. Would the chilli have prepared him for the fiery struggle being waged in his body? He would never know. Just like he would never know about the anti-narcotics officers waiting for him at the airport after a tip-off just hours before his plane was due to touch down. Nairobi had been identified as a notorious route for narcotics from Asia into Africa and further on to America. Beginning to rival Jo'burg. The Americans were putting pressure on the Kenyan authorities to clamp down, and clamp down hard. Incentives and financial rewards were offered. Trade concessions. Training. Technology. The magical Amelica dollar changed jurisdictions. So-called logistical support up-graded.

A new era of cooperation. Allies united against unseen and forever-mutating evil empires. You're either with us or against us. New polarities charted out, battle-lines re-drawn, old enemies welcomed with open arms and new ones created in their place. The war against terrorism exposed Kenya's vulnerability in the new global *dis*-order. The bomb blast at the US embassies in Nairobi and Dar changed everything. This was no child's play. Weapons of mass destruction. Drugs of mass intoxication. Ba-yo-logical warfare. Far cry from ba-yo labs for teenage boys dreaming of massive fun with scantily-clad ba-yo teacher.

Karani walked into a spider's web, like an innocent, timorous fly, never once imagining how he would be devoured, but always suspecting the plan wasn't as watertight as Olu claimed. Now it was too late. *Leave it with me.* The plan left out some crucial caveats.

'What a wasted opportunity!' growled the commanding officer. Operation Thai Spicy Soup wasn't going according to plan. The soup was ruined.

His colleague nodded. He understood. It wasn't about all the money that would have been made had the deal gone through. No. Now the mule wouldn't lead them to the big-time dealers. The godfathers in New York, Bangkok and Lagos who put together the deal, the contacts in Nairobi and a host of other cities. They had been closing in on the syndicate. Cooperation was beginning to bear fruit at last. Or so it seemed. This was supposed to be a breakthrough. The sting that drew blood. We'll get them. Roger that! Chah Lee lost his deposit, but lived to fight another day.

The events of the recent weeks flashed through his tormented mind before he sank into full oblivion. *Leave it with me. This is our big break.* The persuasive gestures that brushed apprehension away and won him over. Now they were dealing him thunderous blows on the head. Blue flashing lights shone on the angelic face of a little chicken. *You go with me? You hel me? The pellets sat on the table. Time to swallow. Mai mee panhaa.*

Internal combustion firing up with peristaltic motions. Bayo gone mad. The promise of passion. Mass amusement. Mass destruction. Or just a myth. A fine dream to keep the gloom away, but the lights went out.

The dream went out.

London Slaves

Barely three hours after leaving Leeds, I make my way through the main exit at Birmingham New Street and into the crowded lobby. It is 3.30 and the sun is shining over the buildings across from the short-stay car park. The air is filled with announcements about train delays, departures and arrivals. But mostly about delays. They always have delays on British Rail. It seems so normal that no one complains. In fact no one seems to think it's unusual.

When I was on the train as we approached Birmingham the ticket inspector caught a guy without a ticket. The guy complained that it was the fault of British Rail that he didn't have time to buy a ticket. The problem was that the train arrived on time. The trains are always late, and that's why he always had time to buy a ticket. Everyone thought it was hilarious. The inspector had one look at the guy, lips tightly squeezed together, eyes unblinking in a murderous look. For a moment I thought he was going to smash the ticket machine on the guy's head. All he did was issue an on-the-spot fine.

Kimani is nowhere to be seen. He had said 3 o'clock. I suppose he's still on what we call 'African time'. If he's going to be doing any business in England, he'll have to stop this tardiness. I can just imagine him making an appointment for 2 p.m. and showing up an hour later, with a silly grin and some feeble excuse about a taxi driver who didn't know the way. It's always someone else's fault. He'll probably blame me for his lateness, claiming I didn't give him proper instructions.

I still can't get over the thought of Kimani coming to England. I've heard he has become a regular tycoon, and I can't wait to see how the former junior office clerk managed such a feat. When he first called to tell me, I assumed he was just showing off, which is common amongst my Kenyan friends. They call you from their office in Nairobi and say, 'Hey, I'm coming to London. Let's catch a few pints, yeah?'

Kimani called from Heathrow and said he was staying at the Campton.

'Campton? Where is that?'

'You don't know? London is so big? I can't believe! Wait, is written here, Broad Street, Birmingham B something-something.'

Kenyans seem to think the UK is as small as Nairobi where everyone knows the names of all the little hotels. And no matter how often I tell them I don't live in London, they still insist on calling the whole of this country London.

'I'm in Leeds, actually. Up north.'

'North London? There's tube station there? What name?'

There's no real reason for me to travel all the way from Leeds to meet Kimani, simply because he wants familiar company in a foreign land. He and I never got on together at the office. He was too much of a bootlicker for my liking. Maybe that was the only thing he knew, the only way he could get anywhere. As a junior admin staff with little education, he couldn't compete with the economist heavyweights.

Anyway, I'm hoping he remembered to bring me some Kenyan newspapers and a packet or two of maizemeal which you can't find here. The alternatives in Indian corner shops can't beat the real thing. The *ugali* ends up elastic and sticky, like plasticine.

At Birmingham New Street, I stand near the entrance and watch people come and go. Every few minutes after a train arrives, a wave of people surges through the exit and heads out into the city, buttoning their jackets as the chilly wind wipes the smiles off their faces. It's already spring, but the sun never seems to get any warmer than I remember it last autumn when I first came to England.

I walk towards the phones, and then decide against it, in case Kimani's on his way. I walk over to a patisserie. Just looking at the cakes and pastries is enough to make my mouth water, but the prices keep me rooted to the spot. A small jam tart costs the same as a plate of chips at the office canteen. It's a quarter past four and there's still no sign of Kimani.

Eventually I walk to the telephones and look up the number of the Campton in the phone book. Kimani answers immediately, his voice loud and boisterous. He has been drinking. He has the TV on so loud I can barely hear him.

'Shege! My friend. You've arrived?'

'An hour ago.'

His laughter reminds me of the frenzied chatter of monkeys. I hold the phone inches away from my ear, and struggle to remain calm.

'So fast, my God! English trains, my friend, not like Kenya bus, eh? You can't believe!'

'I'm at the station, Kimani. Are you coming to meet me?'

'Is okay, my friend. You come here. My hotel near-near station. Walk five minutes. I wait for you in lobby, eh?'

A lady at the customer help desk gives me directions. Kimani is not waiting at the lobby. He ushers me into the biggest hotel room I've ever seen. It's the epitome of opulence, from the king-sized bed to the well-polished furnishings including two leather sofas and a wide assortment of wines and spirits lined up in the mini-bar. I have a view of the entire city centre. Old majestic buildings which I assume are museums, City Hall, and Crown Courts. I turn down the volume on the TV which is showing a Premier League match.

Kimani keeps calling me 'my friend'. I don't know if he has any friends at the office. After he got promoted to office manager in dubious circumstances he started to run the office like a personal fiefdom. But it's funny how even sworn enemies become drinking buddies when far away from home.

I marvel at his designer suit and red silk tie. He could pass for a minister. I've heard rumours about his contacts in high places and new-found wealth. In this era of rampant corruption in Kenya, overnight riches are the norm. Those who are not doing it are just biding their time, like fish waiting for the juiciest worm before succumbing, almost inevitably, to the bait.

'Shege, I'm in London. We need show whitemen we black

people also have money, eh?' His booming laughter fills the room like a clap of thunder.

He sees me eyeing his brown leather sandals. I'm unable to hide a frown.

'My sandals? Oh, Shege, I know is shame. Very shame! But I tell you, when money come knocking your door, sometime you have to pay price. Hah! Hah! Hoh! Hoh!'

'What price is that, Kimani?'

'You see, Shege.' He grabs me by the shoulder and whispers, 'when money come knocking your door, eh? Life not so easy. Gout, my friend . . .'

'You have gout?' I've always associated gout with rich politicians and businessmen. That's when the enormity of Kimani's new wealth and status hits me.

'Well, my friend,' he says, laughing, 'it's not . . . you know . . . I don't quite . . . thing is, sometimes my feet too much pain. I know is gout. It's coming. When you in my shoe, you know. Rich men problem. Poor student like you don't understand nothing.'

I recoil and stand by the window. There's no need to disclose that I didn't come here to study.

That was just an excuse, a way to get out. I couldn't stand the stress at the office, the bullying, doors slamming in your face, everywhere you turned. We just can't seem to get it into our heads that it's not what tribe you belong to, but how you perform. But we cling onto this thing called tribe, expecting, no, demanding that tribesmen throw favours our way. Celebrating when one of us gets a top-level appointment. As though it was a triumph for the whole clan. We never seem to realize how quickly the lucky ones forget us once they've passed the threshold and moved on. My job in the Social Services here might not be the best in the world, but it doesn't come with all that baggage.

From the eighth floor, the city is quiet and serene, and for a brief moment, I'm able to shut out Kimani's incessant chatter and admire the view. That is, until he asks what I want to drink. I'm happy to have a beer, but he won't hear of it.

'Wine, my friend!' he exclaims. 'Forget your student problems. This is the life. In Kenya they have useless wines. Look at this. Bordeaux. French, my friend. White people know how to live. Not like us. We don't know nothing. Even we have money, we missing something. When we gonna catch up, eh? Tell me.'

I listen to him in silence. I heard this kind of talk all the time in my village when I was growing up. The way white people behaved was always held up as a standard for the rest of us. I tell Kimani that white people are just like us. I've been here nearly nine months. I ought to know.

I pick up the bottle and study the label. I learn nothing from it, except that it has a distinct touch of class I haven't seen on any of the bottles at my friends' parties. Being a beer drinker, I don't even know what I'm supposed to make of it. The name Bordeaux sounds familiar. I've heard it on cookery programmes. But the rest remains alien. Cabernet Sauvignon. Merlot. Medium-body. Fruity aroma. Appellation Contrôlée. Château la Lagune. Haut-Médoc. I end up admiring the print of an ancient castle.

'Aged in oak. What does that mean, Kimani?'

'You're so lucky,' he says, ignoring my question. 'Living in London. You have everything. Good wine, fast trains, smooth roads, clean building. What more you want? And there's no corruption. Is perfect.'

No corruption? He has probably never heard of the word sleaze, which I see repeated on every newspaper page. It's always Tory sleaze this, Tory sleaze that. And Kimani's a fine one to be complaining about corruption. From what I've heard, he has greased everyone's palm, from the police and judges to Central Bank officials. But I don't get a chance to challenge him on this. He's on the phone.

'Room service? Come and open wine for us, eh? . . . okay.'

I look up in alarm. 'There's no need to call them, Kimani. I can open it.'

'Wait, wait, my friend.' He leads me to a seat. 'How often white people serve me in Kenya, eh? You see whitemen in Kenya how they have slave mentality? You go every restaurant. White customer, black slave, eh? You can't believe!'

'Kimani, you can't call waiters slaves!'

'But white people in Kenya, old colonials, you know. They have slave mentality. They forget Kenya is free country now. Is too bad. You can't believe! Is our time to eat now, and still they treat us like slaves. I can't accept.'

42

'But the workers themselves, they're . . .'

'Shege, these people refused to go school, eh? They say education is not underwear. They're stupid. Me, I struggle. Even my father don't have enough money for fees. And people look me down. They laugh, and say high school drop out! Still I work hard. I don't want to be any slave for nobody. Now I run my own business. And I can afford come London for business. Buy machines, cars and computers here. I quit job. I'm myself boss, you know? And the slaves who laughed, now they come to me, beg me for jobs, for money! Haah! I'm man of action, not theory like your studies.'

'You've come a long way, Kimani. I can see that.'

'Now you understand. Now is my turn to enjoy. You know what our people say, the man that serves is not prevented from being served later. Chance comes later, eh?'

He puts his feet up on the magazine-littered coffee table and, pointing at his sandals, declares, 'They can kiss my boots!'

He sits back and bursts into laughter.

'You look like a king, Kimani.'

'Shege!' His face lights up. 'You can call me King Kimani the First. I'm now ruler of London. Hah, hah, hah! Look, Shege, you know how many people in Kenya can stay this kind hotel, eh? Nobody! But now we change roles, you know? White people serve me. You can't believe! Heh-heeh!'

'They serve me all the time, Kimani. It's nothing special.'

'You're lucky! For me, is new feeling. I want white slave serve me!'

He gets up, rushes to open the door and keeps it ajar with an ashtray. Then he stands in front of the wall-length mirror, adjusts his tie, turns to admire his suit, and resumes his seat. He selects a cigar from a leather-bound box on the coffee table, lights it, then sinks back into the seat, a hand behind his nape.

'Hey! Kimani, you're quite something.'

'Let these white slaves know they're dealing with who, eh?'

Four minutes later, the doorbell rings and a waiter pushes the door open. Kimani's face falls when he sees a tall black man walk into the room. The man stifles a frown as he picks up the ashtray and shuts the door behind him.

'Evening, gentlemen. Will this be the wine, sir?'

'Mmh-huh,' murmurs Kimani through a cloud of cigar smoke, as if trying to hide his face.

The waiter pours a little for him and stands back.

Kimani looks up at him, puzzled. 'Pour more, pour more!' He's waving rapidly with his cigar-laden hand.

After the waiter leaves, Kimani leaps to his feet and bangs on the coffee table, nearly knocking down the wine, his face distorted with anger.

'Impossible! You see how they treat me? They don't even send me white slave! Why? You tell me why!'

'Most waiters in these sorts of places are black, Kimani.'

'Nonsense! How come I see white slaves in restaurant, eh? Yesterday. Is just discriminate against us because we're black. Why they send me black man? If I want black slave to serve me there's too much in Kenya. I can't believe! They think white slave cannot serve black people! How can you live in this country, Shege? Is discriminate!'

Kimani only starts to cheer up after we've worked our way through two bottles of wine. He looks up at me, cigar between his lips, and says, 'Hey-hey-ehh! The life, my friend! You see how that slave call me "sir"? They see me and now they know who they're dealing with.'

'Who?'

'What do you mean! Sir Kimani Benson, the King of London.'

A Glimpse of Life

As I cross the road to print the latest chapter of my dissertation at the cyber café in the mall, my cell phone rings. It's Huiqing. She sounds agitated, as if she's about to burst into tears. My heart sinks.

'I need to see you, Kalenga, as soon as possible,' she pleads, the words punctuated by a series of gasps.

'The earliest I can get away is five, darling. Aren't you at work?'

'I'm at home. Afternoon off.' Is that a sob? Could she be crying?

'Is everything alright, darling?'

'Let's talk. When we meet. Please hurry.'

The exchange lasts no more than a minute, but it leaves an unsettling emptiness deep in the pit of my stomach. I've never heard Huiqing sound so distressed. Has she been fired?

It's only a little after two. Whatever it is, I know it will trouble me all day and I won't concentrate on my writing. It's better to go see her right away. The graphs I was planning to prepare will have to wait. I hope the computers in the engineering department won't be too busy tonight.

Huiqing and I have been going out for a year. She is a financial executive for an American investment firm, the type that have been mushrooming all over Shanghai these last few years to serve the Chinese nouveau-riche and the expatriates who are sent out here to teach the Chinese modern business practices.

Some of my African friends say I'm crazy to be dating an older woman when the campus is crawling with pretty twenty-year olds. Others think it's perfect, imagining she's like Sandy Lin, the professor in our department who was once married to an American English tutor. The rumour is that she now raises their son on her own, making no demands on the father.

For a long time I didn't have the courage to reveal that I was married. And Huiqing didn't ask. She has never been married.

'Kalenga,' she said, holding my face in both hands, 'I don't expect a guy your age to be single. Late thirties? No. I've always felt you have a family and will go back to them when your work here is done and you're finished with me. So let's not pretend.'

I had no idea how to respond to such disarming candour. But I feel sad for her that she's still single, at forty-three, although you couldn't tell that simply by looking at her. She looks twenty-eight. That's the thing about Chinese women. They look perpetually young. Huiqing says it's the fresh vegetables, fruits, soya sauce and green tea. It will be difficult for her to find a Chinese guy with whom she can raise a family. The guys here like them young, in their early- to mid-twenties, just like back home. She'll probably end up with a white guy, like some of her friends. Once I asked her whether she thinks I might be wasting her time. She said if she meets someone suitable, I'll be the first to know. At first I was shocked, then relieved.

After printing the document, I get on the minibus to Huiqing's flat in Hongqiao. It takes half an hour to get there in the heavy mid-afternoon traffic. I try not to think of what might be troubling her because no matter how much I rack my brains, I cannot imagine what it could be.

When I saw her three days ago she was as cheerful as ever. Okay, so she moaned a bit about the heavy work load. And she's probably worried about her Chinese New Year bonus. Did she fail to reach her target? That's unlikely. Her whole life is devoted to her work, achieving impossible targets, extending her client base, filing monthly reports, making money.

She opens the door as soon as I ring the bell, and throws her arms around me, sobbing into my shoulder. She's shaking so much I'm afraid she's having a fit. I try to comfort her but she's inconsolable.

Eventually I manage to hold her chin up and look into her eyes.

'What's the matter, darling? What happened?'

'It happened!' she gushes, and quickly buries her face in my shoulder again.

'What happened? Talk to me, honey. What happened?'

'I went to see the doctor yesterday evening, Kalenga. He confirmed it. I missed my period, you see . . .'

'You missed what?' It is my turn to tremble. 'How is that possible, Huiqing? We're always so careful . . . I can't believe . . . are you sure?'

She's recovered her composure just as surely as I've lost mine. She leads me to the leather couch where we've made love countless times before. She sits on the carpet and grabs hold of my damp hands. In a daze I glance past her at the potted plants on the balcony, wondering how she could be so mistaken. She told me she couldn't have children.

'The first time I ignored it. I thought it's a change of hormones. The second month I got worried.'

It's conceivable. When I look back, I can think of times when we were so intoxicated I might have rolled over her, in the middle of the night, made love and only remembered to take precautions in the morning when the alcohol and bhang had worn off.

'The first doctor was so wrong, darling,' she's saying. 'All these years. I should have got a second opinion. But now I just don't know . . .'

'Are you sure about this?'

'There's no mistake. I was so shocked I just came back home and sat here, thinking what shall I do?'

'You didn't call me . . .' I mean it merely as an observation, at worst a mild lament, but to her it comes through as an accusation. She shakes her hands in frustration and turns away from me in indignation, biting her nails. I slide down to the carpet and put an arm around her shoulders. 'I'm sorry, honey. It's just that this whole thing has just thrown me, you know?'

She turns to stare into my eyes, as if trying to figure out if I really understand what this means, which I do, but only partially. I know for example that she's not ready to have a child, with me or anyone else. She would have to be married first. But there's no one on the horizon, except me, the quite unsuitable black married lover.

Her conservative parents who are farmers in Anhui would never understand or accept the idea of their only child raising a child on her own, and a black one at that. I have seen enough such kids here to know that they would look more black than Chinese. My Tanzanian friend Rashidi has a Chinese wife and two kids. After his masters degree he got a job with a construction company and has made China his home. There's very little Chinese about his two little boys. They look like the Swahilis from East Africa. But at least they have a father to protect them and explain to them why they're so much darker than their friends.

I won't be here to raise and protect this child. Would Huiqing be able to raise a black kid on her own, in this society where black people are known as *hei gwei*, or black devils? I turn to look at her teary eyes and something in me dies.

'I know it's a shock, sweetheart,' she says, 'but can you see what this means? I *can* have children! What other proof is there? I'm pregnant!'

Her eyes are filled with a dazzling, triumphant glint, and her face beams with delight. I'm momentarily shaken, once again.

'But, honey, how . . .?'

The words are left unsaid when I see her eyes fill up with a steely hardness that matches the stern expression on her face. I've never seen her like this before. She looks so much older than her perpetual twenty-eight years.

'As a man you can't understand this. To you, it's simply a problem. But hey, don't worry, I'm not going to get you into any trouble. I can handle this on my own. I don't need your help.'

Her stinging remarks and her demeanour make my insides cramp up. She makes it sound as if I don't care if there's a child growing up in China believing cowardly daddy ran away back to Africa, unwilling to face up to his responsibilities. She thinks I can simply walk away as though nothing has happened, because that's the easy option a girl expects to see a man take.

I don't know how to make her understand that it's not that simple.

I get up and walk to the kitchen to fetch two bottles of Tsingtao and return to find her smoking. I'm about to tell her she has to stop smoking if she's going to have a baby, but check myself, and instead watch her blowing smoke in thin narrow jets above her head.

For a long, reflective moment, she holds her bottle without drinking. I drink my beer quickly, as my mind struggles to make sense of this situation.

'Kalenga, can't you see,' she says, watching my eyes closely, as if to confirm that they're open and functioning properly. 'Can't you see this is the best news I've heard in years?' Her hands are clasped as though in prayer. I've no idea whom she might be thanking, the atheist she is. But she's looking particularly grateful for this thing which is now turning out to be a blessing whose significance I haven't grasped yet.

'I'm confused, Huiqing. I mean, I'm thinking how will this work, you know, with your parents, your career, the whole race thing for God's sake?'

'Darling, right now I'm not thinking about problems.'

'What are you thinking about?'

'I'm thinking all these years I've worried myself sick that by working so hard I've messed up my chance to be a mother, like my friend Cheuk Ki. Before they decided to adopt a beautiful little girl, she and her German husband tried for years. She was the one who had a problem. The guy had a kid with his first wife. The job stress, poor health, not settling down when we were younger, all this smoking and drinking, and constant travel. That's what the doctor told her. And out of fear I went to see him too. It turns out he was wrong, honey. I'm fine, can't you see?'

That's when it begins to sink in. She's healthy, she's a real woman, she *can* be a mother. Can? Bloody hell, she *is* going to be a mother, if she chooses to keep it.

I'm lost in my own narrow world, trying to imagine what I would say to my wife and three girls whom I haven't seen for four years. Darling, I'm starting a new family here in China, don't wait for me. Give my love to the kids. No, it wouldn't work like that. I would go back to Zambia, and visit my second family here every now and then. My excuse for coming to China? Business.

It's just a fantasy. Huiqing would never accept such an arrangement.

But there's something else troubling me. Could this be my chance to father a son? When my wife conceived for the second time, we prayed every day that it would be a boy this time. After the third girl we decided to give up trying. Perhaps it wasn't meant to be. It was our fate. We stopped listening to the taunts from disappointed relatives who kept moaning that there would be no one to carry on the family name. My wife put it down to the will of God. As a scientist, I saw it differently. As a man, it was up to me to supply the 'Y' chromosome. Three times, I failed to do so. The clansmen back home wouldn't have understood that. Some said my wife had been bewitched. Their solution was for me to take another wife who could bear sons. Though I feel the absence of a son so keenly it sometimes makes me doubt my own virility, I swore I would love our girls no less than if they had been boys.

'I'm not a stone woman,' murmurs Huiqing, finally taking a sip of her beer.

'What are you talking about?'

'I'm not a stone woman, Kalenga, darling.' She starts to laugh, a gentle chuckle at first, then she explodes into a side-splitting roar that leaves her trembling helplessly, tears rolling down her face.

'And what on earth is a stone woman?'

'A stone woman, darling, is a woman who can't have children. That's what I used to hear women say when I was growing up in a small village hundreds of miles from here.'

I start to *want* to share in her joy. But the reality we both recognize comes in the way, and I merely sit beside her, half-listening to her excited chatter about being fertile, 'like a normal woman'.

Huiqing is definitely not a stone woman. I'm the one turned to stone, mute, uncomprehending.

'Okay, sweetheart,' I manage to whisper, eventually. 'That's good news. *Gan be!*' Bottoms up!

'*Gan be!*'

By the time I leave later in the evening, we've managed to work our way through a bottle of red wine. But our discussion takes us nowhere. The only thing that's clear to me is that Huiqing's infertility worries have finally been laid to rest. She could well be carrying my son.

Outside, it's already dark and cloudy. Although it's only late autumn, it looks like it might rain. The pavement is covered in dead, fallen leaves. There are children riding their bikes in the public square, old people practicing tai-chi. This is my favourite time of year. It's peaceful, quiet, and the sun no longer beats down on you like in the summer.

On the minibus heading back to the student hostel, I think back to the time Huiqing and I first met. Her firm had sent a team of managers to recruit students about to graduate. I saw them wandering about the campus, looking for the economics and finance department, and offered to take them there.

Huiqing was every inch a professional, cheerful and polite to a fault. She asked me if I was interested in joining them when I graduated. They desperately needed people who spoke both English and Chinese. Many of their Chinese candidates didn't speak fluent English. Like all other foreigners, I had to learn Chinese before they let me on the degree programme. I fitted the bill.

I told her I was half-way through my PhD and a job was out of the question. Anyway, she gave me her card and asked me to recommend anyone I thought suitable. I was amazed at just how easy it was to find work in this city. In Lusaka there's no way a complete stranger is going to offer you a job after a five-minute chat on the street, or ask you to spread the word around, unless they're looking for part-time poorly-paid cleaners.

I must admit I toyed with the idea. But it would mean bringing my family here. How would they cope with the heat and humidity in the summer, the freezing winters, the strange language and culture, and the strong smells of stir-fried food, the pig entrails, chicken feet, and unfamiliar bitter vegetables? Where would my daughters study? My clansmen wouldn't understand. Many have not forgiven me for accepting a scholarship in what they dismissively called a poor communist country when I could have gone to the US like everyone else.

Huiqing and I kept in touch, and soon started dating. She said I made her laugh, that I listened to her as if I really cared about what she was saying, as if I genuinely wanted to understand her. She complained that everyone she knew was, like herself, so obsessed with success they had lost the human touch, the ability to see each other as real people. I was touched by her sensitivity, and the way she spoke with such gentle feeling about beauty and music. She struck me as kind and affectionate, living up to the meaning of her name.

She opened my eyes to a world that previously drifted past my solitary student existence like the Huangpu River outside the university, which I only dared to observe from the banks, unwilling to wet my apprehensive African sensibilities. Huiqing persuaded me to wade into the culture, and soon enough I was submerged into Shanghai life like a native.

For the first time I felt truly able to appreciate the different styles of Chinese food, from the fiery Szechuan Kung Pao chicken to the rich variety of Shanghai dumplings and Cantonese dim sum, the different flavours of green teas and their medicinal values, the music, the beauty of their parks, their festivals with dragon dances and red lanterns.

Huiqing had never dated a foreigner before. I was just plain lonely, and she stood out with her intelligent eyes, high cheek bones, long black hair and long legs. I found myself drawn to her big breasts and curvaceous hips that seemed so much more suited to an African woman than the average slender Chinese girl.

She laughed easily, and always seemed so cheerful I couldn't get enough of her company. She seemed free and independent, and stayed out late with me, drinking and smoking, and playing pool at the trendy foreign-themed pubs near the Bund.

Sometimes she took me to parties organized by expatriate marketers, IT and financial experts who described themselves as recreational substances-users. Neither of us could muster the guts to sniff cocaine but occasionally took a few puffs of a joint being passed round. Eyes half closed in a sexy posture, Huiqing would take a long drag and release the thick whitish smoke in circles that danced their way to the ceiling, and I would poke a finger through them as she shook with laughter and the party crowd whistled and clinked glasses, yelling *gan be!*

The following day I call to ask if she has made a decision.

'Give me some days to think about this,' she says.

A few days sounds fine. I too need time to reflect.

Later in the week, unable to keep this thing to myself any longer, I ask Rashidi to meet me for a drink at the Blues Place, the latest addition to the string of watering holes at the popular drinking square off Nanjing Lu. I've been hearing a lot about this bar. A waiter tells us they have DJ musical theme nights that range from Irish folk and Congolese Lingala to reggae and heavy metal. Tonight they're playing sixties classic soul, with a generous repertoire of the likes of Percy Sledge, Otis Redding and Diana Ross.

A few couples are dancing languidly on the circular dance floor at the far end of the bar. Behind the dance floor there's a stage fitted with impressive-looking equipment for the band that apparently comes on at midnight. Huiqing would love this place, if only for the ambience and décor which comprises of multi-coloured lights on the walls made out in the shapes of wild animals, and the ferns growing out of giant flower-pots that line the walls and almost totally obscure the entrance.

'You're sure it's yours?' Rashidi asks as soon as our drinks arrive.

I assure him that paternity is the least of my worries. Secretly, I'm disappointed that's the only thing he can come up with.

'The question is, what's going to happen, man?'

'You could do what the Chinese do, man. Keep her as a mistress. Have a secret family. It's a perfect set up.'

Rashidi has started seeing a girl from his office on the side, that's why he talks like that. But knowing him, I don't think he would even countenance having a child with her. There's no way he could keep it from his wife. Rich guys do it and get away with it, perhaps because the mistress can get whatever she wants and never has to cause any trouble. As if reading my mind, Rashidi says,

'Your wife is thousands of miles away, man. You can keep the two quite separate.'

'No, man, that's not going to happen.'

'Supposing she decides to have this baby, then what?'

I've thought long and hard over it. There's probably not much I can do. The truth of the matter is that Huiqing and I don't have any future together.

I'm trying to maintain a straight face as I field Rashidi's questions, but there's little I can do about the tension that has been building up inside me since the day Huiqing broke the news. This week it has been a real struggle to focus on my work, while I wait to hear from her. Every time my phone rings a tremor runs down my spine.

I have no words for Rashidi. I merely shrug my shoulders and focus my attention on my Tsingtao, allowing the haunting harmonic effects and bluesy rhythm of the Temptations to calm my nerves and put my feet on solid ground.

But it was just my imagination

'It's going to be her decision, Rashidi,' I murmur into my beer.

'Sandy Lin,' says Rashidi, breaking into a laugh. 'Your girlfriend could do a Sandy Lin. You don't need to get involved, my brother. She'll manage alright.'

Will she? I remember how she once explained the beauty of being a single woman. *Who needs a husband when I can make my own money, travel anywhere I like and buy anything that catches my fancy?* As a regional director, she's responsible for a hundred agents. Single motherhood seems such a different proposition.

Huiqing calls me a few days later. Her voice sounds calm and self-assured. I listen for signs of despondency, despair, uncertainty, but there's nothing of the sort. She has spent a week making a decision, with no input from me. It is almost as though I had nothing to do with the conception.

I hold my breath and wait for the verdict, like a convict waiting to know if it will be the death sentence or life. I can see no lighter sentence, for either of us. For the foetus the options couldn't be starker.

'I can't keep it,' she says, softly. 'It's not possible, Kalenga.'

I take a deep breath as the words sink in. The pent-up tension makes my chest heave, as if trying to force it to fill up, like a balloon, to its limit before exploding once and for all, setting both of us free.

'Kalenga? Are you there?'

'Mmh, I heard you, sweetheart.'

'It's the only way.' The firmness in her voice sounds so unlike her. I can picture the taut facial muscles as she struggles to sound resolute.

'Huiqing, have you considered everything?'

I know deep in my heart that it wasn't an easy decision to make. She knows her body clock is ticking. For an intense moment when a searing anger builds up in me, I resent her career and her society for forcing these terrible choices on her. I yearn for a way to reach deep inside the core of the ties that bind us to each other and wrench away this debilitating dilemma they have thrust upon us.

Huiqing's voice jolts me.

'Everything, darling,' she says, the voice softening, with an unmistakable tinge of regret. 'My age, career, my future husband if any, you and me, you know? I know I'm not ready. Not this time. Our relationship, Kalenga, it's . . . you mean a lot to me, but a child? I'm . . . this time, I'm prepared to take the risk that it might not happen again.'

I swallow hard, trying to find my voice. My thoughts fly to Sandy Lin, pushing her blonde-haired two-year old in a pram down the mall, past gawping shoppers snapping pictures of the child with their cell phones.

I admire the way Huiqing selects her words, creating gaps, leaving out the unpalatable sentiments. We know now that she's alive inside. If it never happens again, she'll know she could have been a mother. The little life that will now be extinguished well before it comes into being will always be a reminder. But it doesn't even get a glimpse of life. Not now.

Perhaps it could have been a boy. I'll never know.

The Warrior's Last Job

I walk away from the superintendent's office, my heart weighing heavily on my stomach. *Three weeks' time, Njeru, just three weeks.* That's what he said. But I don't know how much longer I can live like this. It will not be long before my ancestors embrace me.

The super says I'm the best, have been for three decades now. That's why he calls me 'The Warrior'. The young men I've trained are like the discarded scrapings from the sculptor's log. Chickens! They have nightmares for months after a job. They get hauled away for counseling. Puh!

Njeru, they don't make men like you anymore. One last job for my Warrior! Then you can retire for good. The words stay with me all day, like fragments of a song that refuses to fade away.

Makes you wonder, who'll guard the herd when the bull's reign is done? Ngingo Maximum will simply collapse. I was trained in the old school, in the colonial days. The white man paid well for the Mau Mau in the fifties. Now, young people who weren't even born then are digging up graves and calling the Mau Mau heroes; marching up and down the streets of Nairobi. They've no idea what we were up against then. All that terror forged in the forests. With their crude weapons, they were no match for the British. I knew exactly where they were hiding. I led my men deep into the forest, smoking out the Mau Mau. How the British revered me! They knew valour when they saw it. Kenya has changed so much. No fiber at all. Not even in the bravest warders. Chickens!

56

The condemned souls are in the exercise yard, stretching limbs as though to jettison the evil part that caused them to sin. I wonder who it is this time, who is the job, as we say. I sit with the other warders and watch their faces. They know nothing. Not yet. Once people know there's a job going, you'll see the tension in their faces. And feel it in the air, like the fog of death.

The super summons me to his office. It's all good and signed, he informs me. The appeal failed, yet again, as expected. The crime was too heinous.

'It's Mathu. His time is up, Njeru. There's your job, Brave Warrior!'

Mathu's been on death row for ten years. He's from my village. I know his people well. When his lover dumped him, he picked a fight with her husband, and got himself beaten to within an inch of his life. He planned his revenge, waylaid the husband in the bushes and hacked him to death. But, he wasn't satisfied. He dragged the dead man's daughter into a tea plantation and raped her.

She was only five.

'*Revenge!*' he screamed in court. '*I want my revenge!*' Everyone thought he had been bewitched. But the reports said he was fine. Now I'm the man to dispatch him on his last journey.

'Take some days off if you like,' says the super. 'Be here on Wednesday.'

What will I do for a week? Sometimes I don't understand this place. They think time off helps strengthen your resolve, nonsense. When you have to prepare the noose, you prepare the noose. And get the job done. There's nothing more to it.

I can't stand the thought of hanging around Mama, with her nagging and chilli-coated tongue. Sometimes I don't know why I married that woman. Perhaps I'll do some weeding before the rains come. Or, build a new shed for the goats, anything to take me away from Mama. But she'll goad me to explain why I'm at home.

'It's a bit quiet at the prison. They won't be needing me for a few days.'

'Good, you can deal with that tree now.' She's been troubling me about this muhugu tree for years. The tree leans at an angle over the fence, dangerously close to my neighbour's homestead.

It forms a sort of canopy over a disused village path. Nobody knows what's causing it to lean like that. It might be the strong winds we had seven years ago. Mama wants me to chop it down.

'That tree is doing no harm, woman,' I protest. 'I don't want to hear any more nonsense about chopping it down, you hear me?' This is not going to be a happy week.

'If it collapses and hurts Njoka's family, we'll be in trouble. Can't you see that?'

'Leave it alone. It will straighten itself up if it needs to.'

'Tut! Tut!' She shakes her head the way she does when she thinks people have let her down, her face all wrinkled and her eyes rolling like marbles. 'You deal with hardened criminals and don't have the guts to cut down a mere tree.'

'The tree has done nothing wrong, woman! Leave me alone and get back to the house!'

'The headman warned you.' She's standing with hands akimbo, eyes burning holes in my face. 'He's been here a few times this month.'

'Tell the headman he can go hang himself!' I stomp away from her, but not before pushing her out of my way. She stumbles and ends up on the ground, scattering the free-range hens that spend all day nibbling at invisible crawly things on the ground.

I take a walk round the farm to inspect the trees. The loquat fruits are ripening fast. In another few weeks I'll need to bring my grandchildren here to pick the sweet and sour yellow fruits. I head towards the trees by the hedge and stand by the leaning muhugu tree. For five minutes I watch the harmless black ants running up and down the bark of the tree.

This tree has been a part of the family for as long as I remember. My son loved climbing it and hiding in its thick foliage when it stood straight. I don't have the heart to chop it down. It seems to be mourning. Maybe Mama is right. We might be doing it a favour by chopping it down. But, the thought of it fills me with dread. I sit down under its shade and doze away in the hot afternoon.

I wake up hours later and start wandering around, to forget the bad dream. This dream always haunts me when I'm just about to do a job. In the dream I see an old man with a long, sharp knife. He's approaching me, swaying from side to side as though he's dancing, or has a bad limp. I'm sitting on the ground, naked; surrounded by chanting teenage boys. The old man has a sardonic grin on a face tortured by deep wrinkles. He reaches for my legs and spreads them apart with a vice-like grip. Two muscular men are holding me by the shoulders. I start to scream. Someone clasps a hand over my mouth. The old man's face comes closer. It is so close I can smell his breath which reeks of muratina, the sugarcane brew. His knife is raised above my stomach. I can't let him. I can't go through with this.

Summoning all my strength, I raise both legs to kick him away. And that's when I wake up, sweating, always at that point.

As I start to walk down the deserted path, I see a figure approaching, an old man steadying himself on crutches. No one ever comes this way. There can't be many in the village who know about this secluded spot. It is so deserted the path is over-grown with weeds. In fact it hardly counts as a path at all.

When he gets closer I take a good look. It's Mzee Njogu, the condemned man's father. He was Mau Mau. He thought he was freeing the country, yet he has done nothing for himself. When the British captured him, they cut off his leg. He could have got himself killed, and for what reason?

He and I haven't spoken for years. When I last saw him he rambled on about guards and slaves, before limping away. I wonder what he'll say this time. I stand aside to let him pass. He stops and takes a long, hard look at me. Just like me, he has aged. We're no longer the youngsters who used to run around shooting at birds with catapults.

'Mzee Njeru, is it well with you?' His voice is croaky, unsteady.

'It is well. Perhaps you?'

'I am well.' Thankfully, the venom in his eyes doesn't spill into his voice. His voice only has pain, the pain of losing a son who turned out worse than an animal. I look at him and think of all the lives I've taken myself. Every time I hook a noose on a throbbing neck, I swear to myself, this is going to be the last one. But, it's like a bad flu that I can't shake off. It's a curse that follows me around like a faithful mangy dog that no one else will have. It forces me to live like a man whose life is split into two parts which have little in common yet they cannot be separated without destroying him.

All these years I've worn a cloak of lies like a tattered coat in the rainy season. But if I didn't wear this coat, how could I face the people? How could I face my wife, or my seven children?

'How is Mathu holding up?' Mzee Njogu asks suddenly.

What can I tell him? I haven't even spoken to the young man myself. I see him from time to time, in there, with all the rest. There's nothing special about him. I avoid him if I can. What would we talk about?

The crimes he committed in this village have never been forgotten. For a long time his family were treated like lepers. When the village knows this second appeal has failed, peace will return to their hearts. Maybe, they'll start to forgive. The young man's last journey will surely start this time. God can't postpone it forever. The souls of the girl and her father have been restless all these years, casting a curse upon the village. The floods and blustery winds we had three years after the murders were a warning.

Njogu has only one other son, and three daughters.

'I think he's handling himself bravely, considering.'

'Bravely! Where's bravery in this village?'

I look away. When I look up, he's staring straight into my eyes, just like the knife-wielding man in the dream.

'There are too many cowards in our country!'

My whole body stiffens.

'I see this matter of your son has affected you deeply.' I keep my eyes averted.

'You're not listening to me!' he thunders, shaking a finger in my face. 'Too many cowards here. Where are the real men who fought the British to free this Kenya of ours! Hah!'

'You dwell too much on times gone by.'

'Times gone by!' He points at the stump of his leg, hidden in a trouser leg which is upturned and tucked under the belt. 'This loss is not a thing of the past, but a constant reminder of the struggle that still stays with us. You talk of my son. Do you know what pains me? Eh? That boy's cowardly act, what he did to that little girl, and her father. Oh, my people! Where did the blood turn? Did my wife play me for a fool? The devil take him, whoever he is, and his sick son!' He stamps on the ground with his crutch and spits into the hedge. 'Yet, a son is still a son, even though the father is a question to a fool. It's always a question.'

He starts to walk away. A coughing fit makes his head jerk back and forth, like a flunkey nodding to his boss's instructions. He stands still and leans heavily against his crutches. When he stops coughing, he yells 'cowards!' waving a hand like someone trimming the hedge with an invisible sickle.

I watch him amble away. He stops briefly at the leaning tree and casts his eyes over it. He pokes into the tree with his crutch, shakes his head and limps away.

Cowards! The word is still ringing in my ears when I return to the house. Mama is preparing the evening meal. I fetch my gourd of muratina and pour myself a mug. She stops washing the vegetables and stares at me.

'You're starting so early today? Is this how you're going to spend your time now, sitting here drinking all day?'

'You just cook the food, woman. Let me drink my beer like a man.'

'A man!' I can't imagine there are other women in this whole district who talk back to their husbands with such sarcasm.

'Woman, if you have something to say to me, you say it loud and clear, or rest your voice in your head, alright?' I'm tired of her whispers and mutterings. They cut deeper than the words of that clown, Njogu.

Does she treat me with such disdain because I haven't shown her the proof of what a real man can achieve? Oh, how I would love to see her wipe that sneer off her face when she finds out why they call me Brave Warrior. One day she'll discover that I'm not just a warder who shouts orders and watches over common criminals, but the Warrior, and I'm treated with respect. The rest are mere chickens.

'Chickens!'

'What?' she looks up, deep furrows forming on her brow.

'Just . . . just . . . cook, alright?'

We eat in silence. The ugali maizemeal is good, with just the right amount of pepper in the meat sauce. This woman has caused me a lot of heartache, but every time she makes a meal, I forgive her.

'Why won't you cut down that tree anyway?' I can't understand this obsession with the tree.

'Can I eat my ugali in peace?'

'You can eat in peace,' she snaps. 'But, you can also answer me in peace. I told you the headman was here last week, again. I'm just relaying a message. Think about the neighbours. It could crash into their mud hut and kill them all, in case you didn't realize that. Then what will you do? You have money to compensate them? Or you want them to send you to that prison of yours?'

I start to argue that if the tree was going to collapse it would have done so by now. She doesn't give me a chance. Her face is now as taut as a bow. It's the look she had that night, our wedding night. When she made the discovery that poisoned her love. It is a look that she shoots into my face when she wants to poke my heart, like a foolish child poking a hornet's nest with a hot rod. It makes my blood boil.

'You're afraid, aren't you?' Her voice is low, deep and threatening. And when her lips begin to curl downwards, I know I'm not ready for this. I push my plate to the earthen floor and head to the door. Her next words bring me to a halt. 'Afraid of anything that involves cutting, eh?'

I turn round to face her. This is the farthest she has ever gone. I feel we're wading in crocodile-infested marshes now. I can almost see the animals' gaping jaws. And I am scared. I don't think she is. I'm looking at her face, my mouth wide open, begging her with my eyes to retreat to safety. But she's not listening to me. She's not even looking in my direction. She's looking straight into the fire, at the low-burning flames that seem to fuel the fury in her heart.

'You heard what I said,' she whispers, as though afraid to wake the demons she's tucked away all these years.

'What are you trying to say?'

'You know what I'm saying! You know what you are. And what you're not.'

Instinctively I glance over my shoulder. But there's no one else here, just the two of us. Since our youngest left home ten years ago, it has been just the two of us, a man and his woman. Each knew and understood. But did we really know our roles?

'I faced the knife!' she spits out the words I've been dreading all my life. Then her voice drops to a whisper. 'I faced it, without a tear in my eye. Just like our people require it. I left the dirt and grime of girlhood behind me. I was made whole. A *woman*.' She breathes 'woman' with a hand raised as though in victory. 'But you . . . you were not true to me. You ran from the circumciser! You chose to remain unclean, against the traditions of our people.'

I sink back onto my three-legged stool, my legs drained of energy as my heart throbs with a mixture of fear and anger. The warrior just had his spear and shield taken away from him. Who put her up to this? Could it be those mothers' union church women? This headman she keeps yapping about? Does *he* know?

'Who gave you a son and six daughters, woman? Tell me that!'

'Let me educate you. Even an unclean teenage boy can impregnate a woman! It doesn't make him a man. Anyway, I only wanted four. But you had to put me through all that pain. *I want a son! I want a son*, as though my womb were a baby factory!'

'You know what a son means to a man, woman!'

'You did not come to me as a man. So don't you dare talk to me about sons and men!'

'Thirty-five years, Mama,' my voice is no louder than a croak. 'Thirty-five years we've been married. Why this talk? Why does it matter now?'

'Because for thirty-five years I've been the real man in this house! And all I get is abuse, beatings, humiliation. I did not endure the knife for this pain.'

'I paid cows and goats for you, woman. You cannot talk to me like this!'

'So now you think you can treat me like a cow, eh?'

It happens very quickly. A force I barely understand consumes my being and sends me flying across the hearth, knocking down Mama's clay pot and spilling the goat stew with just the right amount of pepper into the fire. The fire cackles into life, unsure how to deal with this unusual fuel. Meanwhile, my hands are wrapped like a noose around Mama's neck. I see her lips move. But the voice I'm hearing is saying: *You're The Warrior!*

Just do the job! You're the Warrior! The rest are chickens! The voice seems to be coming from deep inside my head. But it's the super's voice.

The old man fills my head. His knife is coming down. Down! Down! They're holding me down like a sacrificial lamb. *No! No!* My fingers go numb. Mama is coughing, gasping for breath. I grab the gourd of muratina and stumble out of the door.

This devil that has consumed me will not let me rest. It has been trailing me all these years, hovering above me on every job. Forcing me to shut the rest of the world out and show them who the real warrior is. It won't leave me alone. The two parts are coming unstuck at last. Will it be a crime if The Warrior makes a choice? My hands have done this before. I look at them and smell the choking stench of shame. How can I face Mama?

The Warrior is fighting unknown foes tonight, under the moonlight and the winking stars swearing me to secrecy; while the goats sigh and snort, unsure what to make of their guest.

I wake up at the crack of dawn. Under the weight of a hangover so heavy it takes me a good ten minutes to realize the sleepy eyes glaring at me are those of my goats. They seem to be asking what about that new shed? I'm still holding onto my gourd, which now lies empty and exudes the nauseating smell of stale beer.

In my muddled mind, I sense Mama's eyes, flashing like searchlights chasing after retreating escapees. I've seen men try to escape before, jumping over the broken glass-topped high wall. This has to be my turn. But, it is a different form of escape. For how does the warrior run from himself, from the enemy within? I stagger to my feet and untie a tether from the shed gate. Deep in my heart I know the leaning muhugu tree is beckoning, and now I know why it leans like it does. It's mourning for us, and for itself. And for the fallen warrior; the warrior without his spear and shield. I can feel its call in my shrinking bones. And I know there's no other way to appease Mama. It's the craft I know best, my work all these years, unbeknownst to her. My hands might have caused me shame last night, but they'll deliver me yet from perdition.

I pick up a ladder and hoist it up to my shoulder.

What does he want here now? Why is he scanning my trees as if he wants to mount them like the black ants?

'I want to buy this here timber,' Mzee Njogu announces even before we exchange strained greetings.

'The tree is not for sale.'

'It was a tree just like this one,' he mumbles.

'What are you talking about?'

'A muhugu tree.' He pokes the tree with his crutch. 'Karimi. I see you've forgotten him. Huh! Even a fool can bury the truth alive. But the grave is like the hollow bamboo forced to detain a restless cricket.'

My head is spinning. I lean against the ladder and stare into the skies. The sun is emerging over the horizon. You can see it moving, getting bigger by the second. The noises of the morning shatter the solemn innocence of dawn.

'You think I haven't known all these years? Was it the money?'

I shake my head and refuse to sip the condemnation from his eyes.

'He was our dear friend, Njeru, when we were boys growing up. Have you forgotten? He risked his life to look for you in the forest when you got lost, running from the British, before you started to do their dirty work for them. Karimi searched for you all night, until he found you hiding in a porcupine's lair, shivering with cold. And what about that day you fell into the dam? You couldn't swim. No one could, except Karimi. He swam out there and got you out. And then you did that thing to him. He was a freedom fighter! A truly brave man, freeing us from the white man's terror. I know, for I was with him in the forest. What did the white man give you that is more precious than the love of your own people?'

'I have paid for those sins, Njogu. You have no right to dig them up now.' My voice trembles, tears scorch my eyes. I look away.

'You're the experienced one. You'll handle my boy right.'

'I can't touch your son. I'm resigning. This is the end.'

'What does it matter, puh!' He bursts into laughter, and ends up choking on his cough. 'If you don't do it, someone else will. Your government knows how to do its job.'

'There's only one job I have to do now. And I want you out of here!' I push him away. He's stronger than I had expected, in spite of his missing leg. We face each other over the ladder. Our eyes locked together like the horns of two bulls fighting over a heifer.

'You were right, Njogu,' I growl at him. 'There are too many cowards here. Let the men stand up and be counted!'

'It's too late for you now. I did not see you at the river, Njeru. Where all the raw, young boys assembled, waiting for the old man with the knife.'

My grip on the ladder tightens.

'What . . . What are you talking about?'

'Oh yes, we gave you the benefit of the doubt.' He waves a hand, as if swatting a pesky fly. 'The white man turned our lives inside out. People sent to prison. Families broken apart, sent to faraway districts. Yes, Njeru. You could have been anywhere. Running from the knife was not inconceivable in all that confusion.'

My hands are shaking so furiously I'm afraid I'll break the ladder before its job is done. And then I'll surely have to break Njogu's neck.

'Who else knows?' The voice that escapes my lips is little more than a tortured whisper.

'What does it matter now?' He chuckles. 'You and I are old men. We have sired many children, you too, irrespective. Who would have thought? As raw, unclean boys we never believed it possible to fill up a woman. That's what the elders taught us. You proved them wrong, Njeru. You proved them wrong.' He bursts out laughing, still hanging on to the ladder.

My mind is melting away, like the dew on the grass at the first caress of the sun. I've turned against my own wife. How can I live with myself? How does The Warrior set himself apart from the jobs he dispatches for a living! It's time to end all this.

This is my last noose job.

'Mathu's yours now. Maybe it will cleanse your soul.'

'He's your son, Njogu. I cannot touch him. Not after every-thing . . .'

'No, Njeru,' he whispers, with a shake of the head. 'Not after what he did. He's no son of mine.'

And with that he snatches the ladder away, lifts it high above his head and hurls it over the hedge into my neighbour's compound. It crashes into their coop. The noise sets the hens clucking in terror and the dogs barking.

'What . . .'

'No son of mine, my friend. And you have a job to do. But not here.'

He jabs a finger into my forehead and stabs a final glare into my face. I watch him wobble away as my knees give and I slide to the ground, grasping at the leaning muhugu tree to steady myself, possessing it till it's truly a part of me.

Random Check

Maina was jolted out of his sleep by the shrill ringing of the phone. He grabbed it before it awoke Polly.

'*Wei*' Hello, he said, with a mixture of irritation and apprehension. There was no answer.

'*Wei!*' He repeated the Cantonese greeting. Still no answer. But he could hear heavy breathing and the sound of traffic at the other end. The call was being made from some busy street. He peered at the caller display, and in the dim light could only make out 'Private'. The number was blocked, just as he expected. Struggling to contain his anger, he replaced the receiver and then on second thoughts, left it off the hook.

Polly was fast asleep. She hadn't stirred. Maina left the bedroom and walked to the kitchen. Without turning the light on, he poured himself a glass of cold water, lit a cigarette and lay down on the sofa in the small living room. A few minutes later, he went back to the kitchen and fetched a beer. After this incident he figured it would be ages before he could get to sleep again. This was the latest in a series of late night nuisance calls during the month. Trying to run a business in Hong Kong was turning out to be a difficult and dangerous preoccupation.

'So now you're really turning the screw!' he lamented as he sipped the ice-cold Heineken and contemplated the burning end of the cigarette in the semi-darkness.

Polly found him slumped on the sofa in the morning.

'I thought you leave for office already, *lougong*.'

He rubbed the sleep from his eyes and tried to sit up.

'Why you come to sleep here, *la*?'

'To think, Polly. I hope you didn't hear the phone last night?'

'No,' she replied, puzzled. 'Again? Is why you leave it off the hook? I just place it back, I hope you don't mind, *la*.'

'You're so lucky! You sleep like a log.' He laughed, in spite of himself. 'They've been at it again. I can't stand this anymore!' He got up, and paced around the living room, breathing heavily and shaking his head.

'Maina, calm down, *lougong*. Please sit down, *la*. It will be okay.'

Earlier that year, a large shipment of electronic goods and machine tools destined for Mombasa went missing, and neither the insurance company nor the shipping agent seemed to be doing anything to help. Maina had been fighting with them for months, while they tossed him around from one office to another. This was supposed to be his biggest break. He was finally going to break free of the grip of unsympathetic financiers and be his own man. Containers did not just disappear into thin air, and he hadn't heard of any ships sinking to the bottom of the sea.

Meanwhile, the creditors who had put up more than half the finance were fast losing patience. So was his bank. This one single event had damaged his creditworthiness so much that it was proving impossible to raise funds for another consignment. The house and office rent had not been paid for two months.

Then there was the on-going saga with Polly's parents. The parents had been opposed to her seeing Maina, a black man, and were at a loss as to what to do now that she was pregnant. And they weren't even married. When he first met Polly, Maina had a lot of misgivings about the relationship because of things he had heard about Hong Kong people.

In his six years in China he had dated local girls but had never imagined tying the knot with any of them. His family would never have approved. And he expected serious opposition from the Chinese side too. He had seen it all too often, amongst his friends. Many were happily married, but for Maina, the cultural differences were not worth the trouble.

'It would never work,' he argued with Ogola, his Ugandan

friend. 'Can you imagine a Chinese girl cooking *ugali*, and rolling up *chapatis*? Or you think I want to eat rice for the rest of my life? No way, *ndugu*.'

'All you think about is food, my brother,' protested Ogola. 'Look on the bright side.'

'What bright side?'

'Well, it will enrich your culture, for a start.'

'Don't make me laugh!'

'So what are you going to do, then, follow Ouma's example and import?'

Maina thought for a while. His friends in Kenya had tried to fix him up with girls for years. But he was never there long enough to get to know any of them that well. He had attempted a few long distance relationships but eventually got weary of the effort. Some of the girls he met couldn't get over the idea that he chose to live in China, of all places. Why couldn't he try America, or even Europe, like everyone else? One girl openly told him she simply couldn't see herself living in *that kind of place, Asia*! Her feelings were coloured somewhat by a cousin's painful experiences in India where he struggled to acquire a degree amidst race discrimination and financial problems, and eventually abandoned it, but not before enduring a nervous breakdown.

'I would rather starve in Africa,' she had declared. 'And I'd do what there, anyway, eh? They have jobs there? I would have to learn Chinese? Give me a break.'

Another girl said she didn't want to live under communism. 'Give me democracy and freedom in the West any time.' She spent a fortune trying to get a US visa.

This was a recurring problem for Maina. Nobody in Kenya understood why he chose to live in China, and later Hong Kong, when he could so easily move to America, or at least London. London was the Kenyan generic name for the whole of Europe.

How's London nowadays?

A puzzled look. *Actually I live in Milan. Edinburgh. Lyons.* Never mind. It was all London.

'My son,' coaxed his mother, 'your cousin is in New York. Are you saying he cannot arrange an invitation for you to join him? That Asia of yours, *ai*! We just don't know what came over you.

We hear they eat dogs and rats. What madness! You've got your degree now, you can move on.'

Maina had been to the US once. The company he worked for in China sent him to Chicago for a month of training. He liked the lifestyle, but he saw very little in the way of business opportunities for what he wanted to do. Trading was what fascinated him. In America, he would have had to get a job, something that didn't appeal to him.

'In the States,' he told Ogola as they sipped Tsingtao beers in their favourite bar in the Pudong area of Shanghai, 'you can drive fancy cars and live in a nice apartment, but for me there's too high a price to pay.'

'Like what? You have a good career, you don't have to flip burgers at McDonalds.'

'As a black man you'll always be a third class citizen, especially if you're from Africa.'

'So how is it different here?'

'Here people kind of leave you alone,' said Maina, with unease. 'Anyway, here at least I can smell out the business opportunities. And you don't get mugged.'

Maina knew at the time he was being naïve. When he moved to Hong Kong and had to travel in and out of town frequently, he felt as though a force beyond him was prising his eyes open, making him realise he 'wasn't going to be left alone', as he had once put it. He increasingly became aware just how frequently he was stopped at the border as he crossed back from the Chinese city of Shenzhen. Once, he was asked to open a newspaper, the only item he was carrying, while hundreds of locals were waved on, dragging heavy suitcases and bulging bags of shopping. The customs officer searched through the newspaper, laying it out, page by page, while Maina looked on, a bemused expression on his face.

'What do you want? What are you looking for?'

'Random check.'

'All these people with these huge bags, you don't think they could be carrying something illegal? What do you expect to find in my newspaper?'

'Random check. Official policy.' Standard answer.

Maina walked away exasperated, wondering what section of

the Immigration Act the officer was quoting from. At the award-winning Hong Kong international airport, whenever he asked the customs officers why they always stopped the black man, that was the standard answer: *random check*. One day, after a tiring flight, he was so angry he demanded to know why he was always targeted.

'This is racism!' he cried, as the officer calmly shook his head and said:

'Is just your thinking.' A few officers had begun to gather around their embattled colleague. Maina glared at them, oblivious of the stares and frowns from Chinese people weighed down by heavy suitcases that seemed immune to 'random check'.

'Look around you! Look at that other black man they've stopped. Why is it that all black people are stopped? Is that random?'

'Is random check.'

'Do you know the meaning of "random"?'

'You can write letter. Complain letter. Up to you.' The officer shut the suitcase and waved him away. Case shut. Dismissed.

The matter of marriage had become like a mantra that everyone in his family repeated every time they spoke or met. He often wondered whether he should follow Ouma's example. Ouma met a girl on one of his trips back to Kenya. They corresponded for a year. Then he arranged for her to visit for a few weeks. It cost a fortune, but as he explained to his friends, it was an investment that was worth every penny. The imported lady liked Hong Kong, even though she had trouble getting work.

Maina started dating Polly to 'buy time', as he put it. He did not expect much from the relationship. He still entertained the hope of meeting a Kenyan on his next trip.

His worst fears of irreconcilable cultural differences were confirmed when Polly insisted on eating *ugali* with chopsticks. He had never seen anything so ludicrous. He couldn't stop laughing. Polly dug daintily into the maize meal Kenyan staple with the chopsticks and carved out a small piece which she then dipped in soya sauce and proceeded to bite into, a morsel at a time.

'What's the matter?' she demanded.

'Can you follow what I'm doing? You eat this with your hands,' he explained.

'Yeeh!' That was how Polly expressed disgust. 'Not so nice.'

'Just try it,' he urged, as he taught her how to wrap the *ugali* around a piece of meat and soak it in the succulent beef sauce before placing it with exaggerated zeal into his mouth.

'Oh, looks disgusting. Like primitive village people. Use chopsticks, *la*.'

They had been dating for almost two years when Maina realised 'buying time' was not quite what the relationship was about. Polly had become an indelible part of his life. He had not imagined it possible that he would fall in love with her. In his mind, he still dwelt on cultural differences, real and imagined, which he believed would come back to haunt them.

What finally won him over was the love she showered on him. She seemed to have refashioned her whole life around his, and to make changes to her life to accommodate him more than he was prepared to accommodate her. She took to calling him by the endearing term *lougong*, old man, which is the way a loving wife addresses her husband in Cantonese. She behaved as though she were born to care for him. To him it was like a throw back to his grandmother's generation. He recalled with amusement how his grandmother was often described as her husband's 'walking stick'.

When he informed his family about her, all the resistance they had always expressed came flooding at him. But this time, rather than rethink his options, he found himself defending her. A few years earlier, this would have been unthinkable.

His father told him he was in God's hands, which sounded more than a little ominous at the time.

It took a long time for him to gather the courage to meet Polly's parents.

'You've brought shame to us!' cried Fong-tai. 'What do you mean you're dating a *hak gwei*?' Black ghost.

Fong-tai did not speak to her daughter for a month. She refused to take her phone calls and totally ignored her when she visited them.

Maina was shocked when he found out. Polly tried at first to reason with her mother, but Fong-tai's mind was made up. Ah-Fong was less hostile, but he too took a while to get used to the idea.

'You must give us face,' said Ah-Fong.

Polly explained that she was a grown girl and could date anyone she liked. For the rest of the week after the fateful announcement was first made, she was testy and restless. Maina visited her at her flat to console her every evening. At that time she was so angry she declared she didn't care if she and her mother never saw each other again.

'And Ah-Mah say she don't want to see you either,' she informed him. 'She said 'don't bring that *hak gwei* here!''

Maina laughed in spite of himself.

'Is not funny, Maina! Not nice she call you things like that! Is too bad, can't you see?'

'Don't fight with your family because of me, Polly. There's no need for you to protect me, sweetheart.'

'So what you're saying? You want to walk away because . . . because of this? Because Ah-Mah discriminate you?'

'No, don't be silly. Just give her time.'

To amuse her and reduce the tension, Maina took to referring to himself as her *hak gwei*.

He would call her on the phone and say, 'This is your loving black ghost!'

At first she couldn't stand it.

'How you accept this kind of treatment? *Chisin*.' Crazy.

'Hey, Polly, what can I do? I see it everywhere. Do you know people on the train sometimes get up when I sit next to them? Do you know I sometimes have a whole seat to myself on the bus because nobody wants to sit next to a black ghost? I'm not going to fight with your mum, Polly. Forget it.'

As she listened to his laments, Polly felt the pain as though she herself were the victim. The thought of people walking away from her as though she had the plague filled her with horror. She wished there was something she could do. But her mind drew a blank.

'Ok, I'll be your loving yellow ghost,' she offered.

'How nice. But it's impossible. To your people, you're either a person or a ghost, right? And if you want to qualify as a ghost, you have to become something else, like white or black. So what is it going to be?'

She began to lighten up and in the subsequent weeks her anger towards her mother abated.

One day he got a phone call from his sister in Nairobi. When he heard her voice his face darkened with alarm. It was too expensive to phone. He immediately knew it was an emergency. Her husband, Macharia, had been car-jacked in the middle of the city as he drove to work. Shocked to see a revolver staring him in the face, he had been slow to get out of the car and the hooded assailant shot him in the head. There were two of them. They threw his limp body out on the street and drove off, firing a few shots in the air. A crowd quickly gathered. Someone called the ambulance.

The injured man lay in a pool of blood in the middle of the road. Passers-by were shocked to see he wasn't dead. The traffic ground to a halt. The police eventually arrived and cordoned off a section of one lane. The crowd melted away. It was no one they recognised. Just another shooting in the city. There would be more car-jackings and fatalities by the end of the day. A few more lives laid to waste in the City in the Sun.

Macharia lay in a coma in the intensive care unit at Kenyatta National Hospital. The family held a fundraiser to send him abroad for specialised treatment. They called all their friends and family abroad. They held prayer meetings, comforted each other, and begged God for his intervention. But they couldn't raise enough money, so they sent him to a private hospital in Nairobi which demanded a hundred thousand shillings even before they could see him.

Maina sent what he could, which wasn't much. He begged them to understand. His family said everything came from God and whatever little he could spare would be blessed. But he knew they did not fully understand. Many thought of him as a rich trader who shipped container loads of goods around the world. They refused to believe him when he complained about the low profit margin after all the expenses and loans had been paid off, and the losses when customers failed to pay. The worst offenders were in fact relatives and close friends, who insisted that debts should occasionally be forgiven.

'It's our way, you know,' a cousin had once informed him. 'It's our way of doing business. Don't you know that? You've lived abroad too long.'

'But this is business! I'm trying to make a living here.'

'I know, but it's also a way to help us. Have you any idea how tough things are in Kenya nowadays? We're suffering, and it's all the fault of this criminal government.'

'You've twice had a chance to vote them out. I guess it's your way, eh?'

'I know. The future generations will never forgive us.'

Macharia was in a coma in a public hospital for a few weeks before he died. Maina suffered alone, separated from his loved ones by a twelve hour flight he could not afford, after the funds he had sent his sister.

The hospital and burial expenses nearly ruined the entire family. Phone calls and email messages kept coming. They begged him to send more money. His brother told him about the things some people were whispering about him, that he had gone abroad and abandoned his people. He had become a Chinese citizen. They said he had renounced his Kenyan citizenship and was going to change his name to something unpronounceable.

The day he got that email from his brother, he was so distressed that at one point he had to stop on the street and lean against a wall. People rushed past him, oblivious of the torment in his heart. No doubt fighting their own battles too. Just another busy day in Hong Kong. People rushing off somewhere, to some appointment, shopping, to clinch a business deal, make some money. Chatting loudly on their phones. Life went on by.

Polly stood by him during the crisis. Although she wasn't a Christian, she prayed with him and did whatever she could to comfort him. She told her mother about it one evening. There was still some tension between the two of them. Her mother remained silent for a long time. She seemed to be having some difficulty making sense of it all, or so it seemed to Polly. But Polly was wrong.

Fong-tai understood alright. She was simply trying to get used to the idea that a world that seemed so alien could suddenly and without warning intrude into her protected existence. An existence that was supposed to be a safe haven from earlier troubles across the border. Hong Kong had been a refuge for many, ever since shedding its identity as a sleepy pristine fishing community.

'It seems like such a dangerous country,' said Fong-tai with bated breath. 'They just shoot you and take your car. Just like that.'

'Maina says it happens all the time. So many guns from neighbouring countries where they have wars, it seems. I'm so afraid to go there.'

'I don't want to hear you talking of going there, you hear me?' At last, confirmation, if any were needed, of her worst fears about the folly of her daughter's romantic interest.

Polly said nothing. No need to fight again. She needn't have worried. The last thing on Fong-tai's mind was a fight. As she reflected on the tragedy in Maina's family, she became more and more morose.

'They shot him and threw him out of the car,' said Polly for the umpteenth time. 'It sounds like a scene from an action movie.'

'It seems there's so much suffering in *Fei Jau*.' Africa. 'Starvation, wars. People killing each other. Or is the TV exaggerating?' Fong-tai was visibly shaken. She fixed her gaze on the television but was oblivious to the game show. Bright lights and musical jingles ignited the audience's anticipation. Someone was just about to win a lot of money. He was getting a lot of questions right. The audience cheered and clapped their hands, faces beaming with pleasure. Sharing in advance the joy of the imminent win.

Fong-tai tried to imagine what life was like in Africa. Gangsters running amok with guns, robbing and shooting people on the streets. She recalled with terror the suffering her family endured during the Cultural Revolution. Her father, a college instructor, a 'decadent intellectual', was taken away for re-education, as they called it. They came for him in the middle of the night. Liu Shauje, Miss Liu, as she then was, managed to escape to Hong Kong with her mother. She never saw her father again. They heard he died of starvation and exhaustion working in the fields. An auntie lost her mind. Miss Liu was so traumatised it took her years before mustering the courage to visit her motherland again.

'Are you alright, Ah-Mah?' Polly saw the wrinkles on her mother's face deepen. Fong-tai was dabbing at her eyes with a tissue. She turned to face her daughter.

'You cannot understand.'

'Understand what, Ah-Mah?'

Fong-tai merely shook her head. They had never discussed her troubled past. It was a taboo topic. Polly knew so little of her parents' past. Fong-tai thought it was better to protect her that way. Where would I begin? The young people today have seen nothing. Nothing like what we went through. The more she reflected on what Polly had said about *Fei Jau*, the more deeply she felt the pain of her family's disintegration.

'I thought we left all this behind. It's strange how the world goes round and round, isn't it?'

Polly nodded, her eyebrows raised. Sometimes Ah-Mah could be so enigmatic.

'The world of Ah-Maina,' Polly looked up with surprise. Ah-Maina. Mister Maina. Ah-who? Normally it was 'that boyfriend of yours,' or 'your *hak gwei* friend.'

'See how his world comes knocking on our door. Reminding us of things we thought we forgot. And *Fei Jau* is so far away.'

Polly gave up trying to understand Fong-tai.

Maina racked his mind long into the night trying to find a way out of his financial woes. He had had to borrow money from friends to send to his sister. The rumours about abandoning his people had stung deeply. With every new debt he dug himself deeper and deeper into a dark abyss from which he had no idea how he would ever emerge.

When he realised he wasn't going to get any sleep he crawled out of bed and went to the kitchen. He cracked a can of San Miguel and sat on the sofa. The next thing he knew, Polly was shaking him by the shoulders.

'Haiah! What's up, *lougong*?' moaned Polly, worry etched all over her face.

'Why you always come to sleep here, *la*?'

'I can't sleep so I come here to think. And then I fall asleep.'
He shrugged his shoulders.

'Oh, too bad. *Neih hou maafan-ah.*' You're too troublesome.
'What's the time, Polly?'

'*Chat dim bun.*' Seven thirty. She looked with scorn at the
empty cans. 'You say you come to think, but you come to drink!
Think and drink same meaning to you? Maybe drink too much,
then have problem to think.'

Exasperated, she collapsed on the sofa beside him, clutching
her slightly distended belly.

'It's not like that, honey,' he coaxed her.

'I'm worry about you, *la.* We have serious money problem?'

He shook his head. 'No, not too serious.'

'So is okay?'

He turned to look at her. Deep down he wondered whether
she really understood the mess he was in. He had tried to protect
her by telling her as little of his business dealings as possible. But
in the last few months, as the pressure piled on, he had begun to
open up a little. He did not tell her about the threatening letters
received at the small office in the mall at Fanling, the unpaid
bills, and the dwindling bank balance. Little did he know it worried her so much she was afraid she would have a miscarriage.

'Yeah, it will be okay, Polly.' He put a reassuring arm around
her. 'But we have to find a way out. I'll go to the bank again today.'

She smiled sweetly as she ran a hand through his hairy chest.
A calmness swept over him as she held him and kissed his neck,
breathing seductively into his ear. Her touch could be so refresh-
ing, and so relaxing, it made him forget his worries, at least tem-
porarily.

'Will you have dinner with your parents tonight?'

'No, I'll come home,' she replied.

He remembered their last visit together to her parents' flat
in Quarry Bay the previous month. Visits to her parents' were
still strained, although Fong-tai had almost completely changed
her attitude towards him. She even took to fussing over him,
constantly urging him to eat more. She asked after his family,
and engaged him in conversations in Putonghua about life in
Fei Jau. It never ceased to amaze her how it resembled the life
she once knew as a girl living in China.

The last visit took place sometime after she announced her pregnancy. Polly and her mother had had a row following the announcement, but during that visit neither parent was saying much. The meal passed off without incident. Until it was time to go.

Maina noted with surprise that Fong-tai remained quiet. Perhaps her husband had cautioned her to act civilly after that row with her daughter. She flared up when Polly accidentally dropped a bowl in the kitchen while helping clear up. It was an inexpensive bowl, nothing to get worked up about. But it triggered off the anger that Fong-tai had kept bottled up all along. With his limited Cantonese, Maina could only pick up fragments of the row. Ah-Fong himself remained quiet. He resigned himself to watching his favourite Chinese drama while he picked his teeth and sipped Chinese wine.

Maina was boiling inside. He couldn't stand the scolding Polly was enduring. But there was nothing he could do about it. Polly had told him on numerous occasions about Fong-tai's temper. Now he had a chance to witness it first-hand. Polly was trying hard not to talk back to her mother, and from what Maina could see, she was doing a pretty good job of it. Eventually, reduced to tears, she scampered from the kitchen and ran into her old room. Fong-tai went on scolding her while she did the dishes.

Ah-Fong was reclining on his rocking chair. While they waited for the storm to blow over, he offered Maina a cigarette. Maina accepted graciously, thinking of it as some sort of olive branch.

Later as they headed back to Tai Wo by minibus, Polly recounted the details of the row. Maina hadn't been too keen to find out because he feared it was all about him. Fong-tai had complained bitterly about the family losing face on account of her out-of-wedlock pregnancy and dubious relationship. And she was an only child! She had also reminded Polly that if they ever got married, they would have to prepare about HK$50,000 for her bride price, otherwise her family would lose face even more.

'I don't understand Ah-Mah,' said Maina when they got back home.

Polly relaxed her hold on him and turned to peer into his face.

'Don't understand what?'

'First she doesn't want us to get married. Then she says, oh, by the way, if you do get married, this is how much you should pay. What's going on here?'

'*Mjih wo.*' I don't know. 'I know for you it's difficult to understand Chinese customs sometimes. The money is not for her, is to buy me things, you know, jewellery and stuff.'

'Oh I understand bride price alright. We have that in *Fei Jau*. Anyway, we don't have money for a wedding. So what are we going to do? I have to give them face, right?'

'Maina?'

'What is it now, honey?'

'I talked to my uncle.'

Maina's heart missed a beat. He lit a cigarette and inhaled deeply. Polly rested her head on his shoulder, blowing the smoke away.

'You want to know what we discuss?'

'I don't want to hear about your uncle!'

'You too proud, *lougong*. My uncle's really nice, *la*!'

Polly's uncle ran karaoke bars in some of the seedier districts of Hong Kong, like Sham Shui Po and Mongkok. He also had links with other amusement establishments which Polly spoke of disparagingly. But she vehemently denied he had triad connections, or anything unsavoury like that. For Maina, the uncle's business dealings remained shrouded in mystery. When he heard how the uncle was miraculously released from police custody in Shenzhen after a business dispute, Maina feared the worst. The saga included an alleged kidnapping, arson at a night club in the wee hours of morning, and police officers being investigated for alleged corruption.

'I'm not accepting any money from that man, alright?'

Polly got up languidly, and without a word, fetched her handbag. She produced a white envelope which she calmly placed on the coffee table.

'We don't have choice, honey,' she said, as she headed to the bathroom.

Maina stared at the envelope as though waiting to see it

explode like a time-bomb. Right here in front of him was part of the solution to his problems. But how could he accept a gift from someone like the infamous uncle? Was this a trick to lure him into shady dealings? Would this be the first drag that turned him into an addict?

He stared long and hard at the envelope. But with his mind in turmoil, he could hardly focus. Instead he saw imaginary words screaming at him in bold, uncompromising Chinese characters. The words seemed to mock him, daring him to reach out and touch them. He thought he heard Polly singing in the bathroom. But the sound quickly changed to the harsh raucous laughter from the bar in Shenzhen where the fateful deal was sealed. Thinking he was finally going mad, Maina jumped to his feet and slapped his temple, as though trying to emerge from a trance. He then reached out for the envelope but his hand froze in mid-air as the phone rang.

'Why you don't answer it?' Polly called out. Maina stood still, as though transfixed to the spot. Then he heard Polly answer the phone. She screamed some expletives in Putonghua and then slammed the phone down so hard it must have damaged the caller's eardrum.

Finally recovering his composure, Maina called out: 'Polly, I can't accept this man's money. Take it back, please.'

Polly emerged from the bedroom, still doing her make-up.

'You think my uncle a bad guy, but you think he worse than those crooks you trade with? Anyway I know you too proud to accept charity. So this is loan. Is cheque.'

Maina shook his head, as Polly reached for the door.

Is cheque. She made it sound like the checks he was more familiar with. The random ones.

'You want breakfast? I wait you at *chahlou* downstairs. Oh, by the way, that money not my idea.'

'Whose idea was it?'

'Ah-Mah.'

Black Fishnet Stockings

Otieno loved the car like his own child. He could sit for hours, while he waited for Mzee, the old man, just admiring the sleek, shiny bodywork. He knew the car very well. When he heard the engine purr, he understood its language in a way Mzee never could. He heard what it was telling him. It spoke in gentle tones, as only a new Mercedes could.

His wife, Selina, had begged him many times to give her a ride around the streets of Nairobi in his precious Mercedes. That's what he called it, *his* Mercedes. But he never let her into the car. He always said the boss would not permit it. He would get into trouble. He couldn't afford to lose his job if Mzee found out he was using the car to impress his wife, or to take her shopping.

'Just one time,' she begged. 'How will he find out? After taking him to work, you're free, just drop by here, one hour, and then go. Please?'

Otieno smiled. 'Okay, maybe one day.'

'Promise? I'll sit quietly, behaving myself. Back left. You won't even know I'm there.'

He laughed. 'I can't promise, but I'll try.' She rubbed his back lovingly and lay back on their single bed, dreaming about the day she would sit in the Merc, back left, while her husband took her on a joy ride, as if it was their own car.

Selina spent a great deal of time dreaming of the good times. On the way to work, she often sat quietly on the bus watching how other women dressed. She watched their hairstyles and wondered where they had their hair done. She herself worked for a hair salon in the city center. Charlotte's Beauty Salon was in an up-market plaza on Kimathi Street. Her job was to wash, shampoo and plait hair. She loved the job. She loved the wonderful things she could do with hair.

But more than anything else in the world, she wanted to run her own beauty salon. She dreamed about the glamorous pictures of famous actresses she would place on the walls. She did whatever she could to get to know the well-heeled women who visited Charlotte's. She knew they were the wives or mistresses of the city bigwigs.

'You never know when you might need these people,' she whispered to her friend Amina. Amina didn't need to be told. She knew a lot of important and famous people in the city. She told Selina she was close to quitting her job and setting up her own salon. She had cultivated contacts with clients who had introduced her to what she called VIPs, very important people. She smiled mysteriously when Selina asked what these VIPs did for her.

For several weeks, Selina begged Amina to let her in on her secret. All Amina could say was that there were many men out there who were only too happy to help a girl in need.

'How do I meet them?'

'You might not have time, Selina.' Amina was single, and unattached. She considered herself free and independent.

'I may be married,' replied Selina, with a naughty pout, 'but I'm not a slave.' She imagined herself making enough money to buy her own car, something chic like a BMW.

'If you're sure, I'll see what I can do.'

'Good girl, I'll buy you lunch today,' offered Selina. They giggled conspiratorially as they walked into the street to their favourite sausage and chips café.

Otieno started the day by cleaning the car, a task that lasted the better part of two hours. He was like a man possessed, to the point of wiping off imaginary specks of dust, and then leaning back to see if any marks were discernible on the bodywork. He was ready to drive Mzee away to the office by eight. He and his wife lived in Kawangware village, only a few miles away from Mzee's mansion on Ngong Road. It took him ten minutes to cycle there.

The guard smiled and greeted him, calling him the magician, for pulling off the incredible trick of coming into the expansive compound in a battered Black Mamba bicycle and driving off minutes later in a brand new Merc.

As Mzee walked out of the door of his palatial home and into the waiting car, Otieno glanced up at the bedroom window and saw the little wave with the index finger beckoning. Mama's coded message. *Hurry back!* Sometimes Mzee needed him all day. So, after dropping him off at the office in Westlands, he would wait in the car park, clean the car and wait to be summoned. If he wasn't needed, he would drive the eight kilometers back to the residence and wait there. He used to while the hours away chatting with the other servants, waiting for the call from Mzee's office.

He liked showing off the new Motorola cell phone Mzee had recently provided him. Gone were the days when Mzee could only reach him by giving instructions in advance. In those days gone by, appointments were sacrosanct. Now, you never knew when you are needed where. Plans could change at a moment's notice.

As he drove Mzee in the early morning traffic, he tried not to glance into the rearview mirror. He couldn't face Mzee. The traffic was a little heavy going down to the city on Ngong Road, but it got lighter heading out of town up Waiyaki Way. Mzee preferred to take that route because it gave him the impression he was going into the city although they actually just skirted round it on Uhuru Highway. The alternative was to drive through the posh residential areas like Kileleshwa. That was the way Otieno drove when he went back to the house to meet Mama.

It had been going on for two months. His affair with Mama. When it first started, it was so unreal he thought he was dreaming. Whenever he took the Merc back, he would ask her if she needed to be driven anywhere. She would inform him if she had errands to run, or wanted to go shopping. So, he would clean the car again while he waited for her to get ready. John, the domestic driver, was responsible for the Range Rover, which was used for taking the children to school. Madam did not like the Range Rover, so she never asked John to drive her, unless Otieno was held up somewhere looking after Mzee. Otieno couldn't blame her. The Merc was in a class of its own.

One day when he brought the car back after dropping Mzee off at the office, he was informed by one of the servants that he was needed in the house. He had never been invited into the house before. He had, over the years, come to enjoy its opulence second-hand, by listening to the two servants and the cook. He had never in his wildest dreams imagined he would ever step through the imposing mahogany door.

'I am wanted?' he repeated, thinking he had heard wrong.

'Yes,' Auma assured him, 'you had better come into the visitors' chambers.' She led him into a large, airy parlour, with curtains stretching from the ceiling to the floor. 'Leave your shoes here.' Auma opened a wall cabinet, reached out for a pair of sandals which she handed to him and then left him standing there.

He didn't know whether to remain standing or take a seat. The leather sofas looked inviting, but he couldn't bring himself to sit down, in case he damaged something. He looked around the room, aware that it was only a waiting room, though it was bigger than his entire house where he lived with his wife, Selina and four children. He did not dare imagine what the rest of the house must have looked like, or just how big it was.

As he was contemplating the carvings and paintings on the walls, Mama arrived suddenly. He stood to attention almost like a soldier and clasped his hands behind his back. Mama was wearing a translucent gown which did a poor job of obscuring her voluptuous curves. Struggling hard not to stare, Otieno averted his eyes and muttered a greeting.

When she walked up close to shake his hand, he took in her fragrance, which was a mixture of a perfume he would never even have heard of and the natural smell of a woman which seeped through her skin as she slept, and then stayed on her skin, as if to remind anyone who needed reminding that she was a woman. It was raw, natural and infused with the suggestion of closeness which made him want to turn around and run away, back to the more familiar ambience of the Merc. He felt guilty about being aware of something as intimate as the woman's body smell so soon after driving her husband off to work.

'You are here.' She motioned him to a seat.

'Yes, Mama. I have arrived.'

'Have you had breakfast?' Before he could answer, she added: 'Have some tea, anyway, while we talk.' She pressed a buzzer on the table. Presently, Auma popped her head round the door. Mama instructed her to serve tea for two. Auma suppressed a sardonic smile as she noticed Otieno's wide-open eyes. 'Listen, Otieno. We are changing our travel arrangements from now on.'

He listened attentively, while keeping his gaze on the beige carpet, and nodding occasionally. Auma brought a tray in and poured for Mama and was about to walk away when Mama passed the cup on to Otieno and asked her to pour another one for her. Otieno saw Auma's facial muscles tighten as she said: 'Yes, Mama. Sorry.' As she was leaving, she stepped on his toes. Otieno winced and bit his lower lip. He sensed she could just as easily have poured the hot tea 'accidentally' on his lap, or worse.

'Here's the new arrangement, Otieno,' Mama continued, as soon as Auma was out of earshot. 'After you drop Daddy off, come back and take me to Adam's Arcade. I'm opening a shop there. I'll need to move around a lot, so you may have to stay with me, and pick Daddy up in the evening later, or maybe John can deal with that.' She had been looking him straight in the eye, but then she started to gaze out of the window to the jacaranda trees outside.

'That is alright,' he said. 'That is good.' He felt some sort of response was expected.

'Mmhh. I'll call for you when I'm ready.' She got up to leave, and tightened the robe around her. He too got up, ignoring her entreaty to remain seated.

'Finish your tea, and wait for me here.'

Otieno didn't dare look into her eyes. He stole a quick glance at her retreating figure after breathing in deep to take in her smell as she brushed past him. He was completely flustered and was left feeling foolish, like a naughty schoolboy. He was still standing there, not knowing what to think when Auma waltzed in, with a sneer on her face.

'So now you're the VIP around here?'

Otieno shook his head, waved her away and walked to the window. But Auma sneaked up behind him and asked: 'So, do you want me to fix you breakfast, mister big shot visitor, eh?' Otieno could only laugh. When she realized he was intent on ignoring her completely, Auma walked away, but not before snapping: 'Let us know if your highness is staying for lunch!'

When Mama returned an hour later, resplendent in a light blue suit and matching headscarf, Otieno felt less threatened by her business-like demeanour and more able to relate to her. He drove her to the premises that were going to serve as her new business. After staying idle for three years following the birth of her third child, she had finally prevailed upon Daddy to allow her to return to work. And this time she wasn't intent on taking any old job. She wanted to run her own business, selling ladies' clothes.

As far as Otieno could tell, the business was doing well. There were always customers to take care of, and Mama talked excitedly about new designs, styles and fashions. Most of these things meant little to him, but he learned to make appreciative noises as he drove her to her numerous appointments. She insisted on asking for his opinion even when it was clear to her, or so Otieno thought, that he was clueless.

He always tried to sound cheerful and never dared contradict her. He gradually became aware she liked him, and little by little, he discarded his shyness in front of her. She told him things he didn't believe he needed to know, about her husband. She tried every trick in the book to discover what he, Otieno, knew about Daddy's trysts with other women.

Otieno feigned ignorance. How can she possibly expect me to disclose such matters! He merely shook his head and remained mute. It was impossible for him to tell her how Daddy often called him on the cell phone to tell him where to pick up some girl, and where to deliver her. Daddy preferred the quiet motels conveniently located around Westlands, and sometimes Parklands, which was only a five minute drive from his office.

Sometimes, Otieno was simply told where to wait. The girl would have been instructed what car to look out for. To kill the time, Otieno played a guessing game, trying to figure out which approaching woman was heading for his Mercedes. He scanned the neighbourhood on his mirrors and watched as girls walked past. Out of the corner of his eye, he took note of the women who stood by the side of the road, pretending to talk on their cell phone while searching for the appropriate license plate.

Sometimes he was caught quite unawares. He would be watching the front or side and the rear door would open without warning and a smiling face would loom in his rear view mirror. The women invariably wore dark glasses. He never got to see their eyes. Sometimes he saw their high heels, boots, or slit skirts as they wandered up and down the road trying to pick up Mzee's Merc.

'*Jambo*,' he would offer a polite greeting.

'*Twende*.' Let's go. A soft reply. And a gentle smile.

The central locking activated, and the engine purring almost inaudibly, Otieno delivered to the designated motel. While the girl made herself at home, Otieno drove rapidly to pick up the boss. It was a well-rehearsed routine. They had done it for years.

There was no way Mama was ever going to find out, certainly not from him. If she wanted to know anything, she could ask her husband. Otieno shrugged and kept his eye on the road.

But even this did not prepare him for what she did next.

'Take me to Ongata Rongai,' she told him. 'I have an appointment there but I'm not sure what time exactly. So we can aim on being there all afternoon. I've told Daddy to call John.'

They drove through Kibera and got to Ongata Rongai half an hour later. Mama had taken care of everything. She instructed him to drive to a motel hidden away behind a thicket of acacia and oak trees.

'This is it,' she declared.

He helped her pick up a bag full of samples. She led the way into the motel, and as soon as they got into the lobby, she sent him back to the car to fetch another bag. While he was gone, she paid for the room she had reserved in advance on the phone that morning.

'We'll wait here.'

Otieno sat in the armchair, and observed as Mama emptied the two bags on the bed, talking to herself the whole time. The idea of getting a motel room to show a prospective customer samples seemed rather strange. Why couldn't they meet in the lobby, or at the customer's place of work?

'Do you want a drink?'

'A soda. Thank you, Mama.'

She reached into her handbag and extracted a two hundred shilling note.

'Go to the bar and get two beers, Otieno.' It was an order.

Mama spoke for the next half hour, mostly about Daddy. Otieno listened patiently. Then she sent him to the bar to get a bottle of wine. He had never tasted wine before. He got drunk quickly. Meanwhile Mama was talking about her business. She asked him if he wanted anything for his wife. He didn't know what to think, and he was certain he couldn't afford anything she sold. So he lied that his wife didn't care too much about clothes.

'Oh, come on,' she cajoled. 'Every woman loves beautiful clothes.' She laughed joyously, and, picking up a bra, asked him what her size was.

He laughed to hide his embarrassment. He had no idea. He told her that as an African man he didn't involve himself in such women's things. His wife would think him strange if he took an interest in her underwear.

She laughed again and tossed the bra at him.

'You're so traditional, Otieno. Men know about such things nowadays, you know? Especially Daddy. He's the expert, isn't he?'

'For us ordinary people, nothing changes,' he informed her.

He glanced at his watch. It was 3pm. He reached into his pocket for his cell phone.

'There's no signal here,' she said. 'You can forget about the phone.'

He felt a shudder of unease go down his spine when he realized his boss wouldn't be able to reach him. What would Mzee think?

'How about stockings?' Mama asked, interrupting his thoughts.

'Stockings?'

'For your wife.'

'Oh, I see. I don't . . . I don't know, Mama.' He shook his head and looked away.

Then he remembered his wife talking about fishnet stockings. Her father was a fisherman back in Homa Bay.

'I saw stockings that look like fishnets,' she had informed him one evening.

'Why are you interested?' he demanded. 'You don't even like stockings.'

'You're so foolish,' she had teased him. 'You don't even know what I like!'

He smiled to himself when he remembered that conversation.

'Ah, I see you're smiling,' said Mama. 'I bet your wife likes stockings. Select a pair. I'll give it to her.'

Shyly, he searched through her samples and selected a pair of black fishnet stockings.

'I'll try them on for you,' said Mama.

Otieno stared at her, open-mouthed, as she got up from the bed, peeled off the brown pair she was wearing and proceeded to wear the pair he had selected for Selina.

God, she's shameless! Otieno gripped his glass of wine tightly and watched horrified as Mama lifted her skirt and showed off her long, slender, light brown legs. Then she danced, languidly, and seductively, with her eyes closed, like someone lost in a fantasy. Otieno felt an inexplicable force take over his being. The force, which he was powerless to resist, gave his previously immobile frame the energy to rise and walk over to the dancing woman. He took her in his arms and together they danced, she with her eyes shut, and he, with his eyes tightly focused on her face.

They danced for ten minutes, without music.

Later as he drove her back home, he replayed the events of the afternoon in his mind. But try as he might, he could not recall the precise moment when the slow dance turned into a romp in bed. All he could remember was that suddenly they were both naked, and although there was no music in the single room, an incomprehensible sense of musicality appeared to have consumed their two bodies. He vividly remembered the moment when she stopped kissing him, reached for her handbag and extracted a packet of condoms.

He had never seen a woman do that before. The embarrassment he thought he had overcome overwhelmed him once more. This time totally. He struggled hard to conquer the sense of guilt that prevented him from rising to the occasion. He needn't have worried. Mama knew just how to light his fire.

He wondered what Mzee was doing at that very moment. Would he have sent John to pick up a girl for him? Was John ever privy to this quiet arrangement or was he, Otieno, the chosen one? He had always envied Mzee, the boss, he of the unlimited amounts of money and the capacity to obtain any woman he desired. Mzee usually gave him a generous tip on those occasions, as though to buy his silence and loyalty.

Yet here he was taking that which belonged to his benevolent boss. The image of Mzee would not leave him even as he succumbed to Mama's wild passion. She was like a lioness on the savanna, anxious to devour a helpless gazelle. Otieno cursed himself for likening himself to a humble, innocent gazelle. Deep in his heart he knew he was more like a hyena, betraying his boss the lion.

He wanted to ask Mama whether her customer was coming at all. But Mama seemed to have completely forgotten about it. Perhaps there was no customer at all. Otieno shivered involuntarily as he realized he was probably the unwitting customer. He couldn't bear to look at Mama. He heard her snore softly as she sat beside him in the luxurious Merc.

The pair of black fishnet stockings in his jacket pocket felt like an oily smudge on the gleaming surface of his beloved Merc. He had put it back neatly in its tiny plastic wrapper, hoping Mama's smell no longer lingered on it. Selina would love it. She had spoken longingly about fishnet stockings but hadn't found any she liked and could afford.

～

For Otieno, the call from Mzee was just a regular call. *Wait outside that new cybercafé on Banda Street, between the bank and that curio shop. 3 p.m. on the dot.* He was there at 2.50, ever the reliable, punctual driver. The man who always delivered, and asked no questions.

He gave up searching around him on the mirrors. There were too many people walking by. He couldn't keep track of them. He saw the low skirt first. The shape of a woman turned from the crowds on the pavement and reached for the door. Instinctively, he released the central locking and she eased herself in. Back left.

He tried not to peer into the rear-view mirror. There was never any need. He always felt like an intruder. He only murmured a laconic greeting. *Jambo*. As he reached across the glove compartment to pick up a CD, he saw, out of the corner of his eye, what looked like a lattice on the legs that stretched out just behind him. Before he could turn his head to see her face, he heard a gasp of horror escape her lips.

And then he saw the lattice more clearly. It was black fishnet stockings. He felt a plaintive voice tear through his troubled mind: *you won't even know I'm there!*

For a Favourite Niece

It's 9 p.m. Kitty's younger sister Lai-Mui must be at home at this time. She never goes out on Sunday. After breaking up with her Canadian boyfriend of three years, her social life just went down the drain. She's even talked of leaving Hong Kong, emigrating to Australia or somewhere.

Lai-Mui is the only chance I have of getting news about my wife's whereabouts. This time I'll beg her if I have to. I take the MTR to Quarry Bay and walk to her apartment block. The thunderstorm warning has been lowered but it's still raining. I never bother to carry an umbrella and by the time I get to her block, I'm soaked to the skin.

The elderly guard dozing in the lobby gives me a quizzical look and stands up to watch me. I'm probably the first black visitor he's seen for ages. I ignore him and press the intercom. Lai-Mui sounds shocked. I've never been to her place before on my own.

Little has changed in her flat since we were last here more than a year ago, when Chacha was four. There's not much furniture here. Lai-Mui says she likes plenty of space to move around. But she spends most of her time slumped in front of the TV, watching Chinese period dramas.

'You alright, Chiponda? It's very late.' She's wearing pyjamas and has a shawl around her shoulders.

'May I use your bathroom?' I dry myself with bits of tissue and return to the living room.

'Something to drink?'

I ask what she has. She brings me a bottle of Heineken. I know she doesn't drink. I wonder what other sad reminders of the soured relationship she's trying to lose.

'Lai-Mui, I hate to barge in on you like this.'

'You could have called.'

'I'm sorry. This whole thing with your sister. I'm going crazy.'

She sighs, and tightens the shawl around her shoulders. Every time I call to ask about Kitty, the answer is always the same: she doesn't want to get involved in our domestic squabbles. But this is no longer just a squabble. Kitty took my daughter away from me. They've been gone almost a year. I can't bear the thought of Chacha forgetting her daddy. And Kitty's whole family just turned against me, like I was a leper.

She was so sweet before, Lai-Mui. When the parents shunned Kitty for marrying a black man, Lai-Mui was the voice of reason in the family, reminding them how they themselves fought for years for acceptance: a conservative Chiuchow man from Guangdong marrying a girl whose Shanghai family could not be ascertained as bona fide.

'Chiponda, you know how stubborn Kitty is. She doesn't call. I've no idea where she is.' I find that hard to believe.

'Lai-Mui . . .'

'It's true, I . . .'

'Alright, alright. She must be with your mother's people? You'll know how to reach them, surely?'

'No.' She laughs and adjusts her shawl. 'We're not like you Africans, extended family and all that. With us, maybe you see them at a funeral or wedding but apart from that, just forget it.'

'Your niece.'

She sits up, blinking. 'Chiponda, please . . .'

'You're her favourite auntie, Lai-Mui.'

'Please, why are you doing this to me?'

'Every time her mother lets her speak to me, she says how's yee-jai? Don't you want to know how she's faring, how she's doing in school? She speaks such good Putonghua.'

'Please stop . . .' She buries her face in her hands.

'Lai-Mui, you've always been the sensible one in this family.'

She starts to sob, and covers her face with the shawl. I wasn't prepared for this, but now I know all I need to know. I thank her for the drink, mumble goodbye and leave the flat.

Fifteen minutes later I'm walking the streets of Wanchai trying to find a bar. I'm vaguely aware of excessively made-up mamasans prowling the pavements outside girlie bars, trying to grab my hand, saying, 'Darlin', one beer? No cover charge.' No, one beer won't do, sweetheart.

I end up at the East Meets West, which is as crowded as usual. The Filipino band is belting out 'Smoke Gets in Your Eyes' as if to mock the patrons gasping in a fog of cigarette smoke. I order a bottle of Heineken and find a quiet spot by the bar, hoping to drown my sorrows in peace.

Who can I turn to this time? After our argument last week I don't know if I can trust Alex. And things aren't going to get any better between us with the latest revelations about farm invasions back in Zimbabwe. I still can't get over my cousin Chipinduka's email. He says my father is heading the band of war veterans who've invaded the farm they work for. Alex's family own a two-thousand acre tobacco farm which is now in the hands of war veterans. Like many other white families, they'll probably have to leave the country. That has made Alex very cranky. I don't know if he's ready to meet me. But he's my last resort. I have to see my family.

I dial Alex's number. I can barely hear him. He says he's in Soho.

'I need to talk to you, Alex.'

'I'm not having any more of that farm crap from you tonight.'

'This is important. It's business.'

'Business? At this time of night?'

'I wouldn't bother you if my life didn't depend on it, Alex.'

'Well, get your arse out here then, eh? We're at the Pirates' Rice Bowl.'

When I get there at 11, Alex is having an argument with Charlie, predictably, about the land issue. This thing just won't leave us alone. It's happening ten thousand miles away in Africa, but it follows us around like a shadow and just won't go away. I get a beer and watch the exchange from the sidelines. Things are getting out of hand.

Charlie describes himself as Black British and proud of it. Pressed further, he'll offer he was born in Cameroon. He has taken it upon himself to educate anyone who cares to listen about the inequities of land distribution in Africa. Our Chinese friends find it all rather confusing. They find it easier to understand stocks and bonds, apartment prices and the slump in the property market that has plunged home-owners into negative equity for the last four years.

Alex insists they acquired their land legally. His family have been living in Zimbabwe for three generations, he claims. So, they have as much right to the land as the Africans. Charlie's having some difficulty understanding how a small minority of white farmers can own virtually all the land in a country which is predominantly black.

I'm not getting involved anymore. And I'm still trying to figure out this whole business of my family acquiring their master's land by force. If the President is going to be in power long enough to protect them, they're home and dry. But I'm not celebrating yet. Not until I've spoken to father. Obiako's the only person I've told about this new development. Two days ago. I didn't intend to, but he was in Harare recently on a business trip and came back sounding very knowledgeable about the whole land thing. Since I haven't been back myself for several years, I found his first-hand experience quite enlightening, and we got into a lengthy discussion.

'The land belongs to the Africans,' declares Charlie. 'Everyone knows that.'

'What do you know?' says Alex, eyes blazing. 'We've all struggled to make that country what it is today. And we're not going without a fight, you mark my words.'

The way this argument is going, I doubt if I'll have a chance to talk to Alex. Charlie turns to me and says, 'So, what do you reckon, mate? This really is your fight, innit?'

'Charlie, I have more important things to worry about right now.'

'What! What could be more important than your land?'

He's probably drunk. He knows very well what I'm saying. I ask him to leave me alone. He curses under his breath and turns to talk to the barmaid. I see my chance and edge closer to Alex.

'What's up? What's this business?'

I'm not sure how to begin. I've only known him a couple of months. And I can't say we've really got on famously.

'Your firm, ahm . . . can they, can you help find someone?'

'Meaning what exactly? We check out potential business partners in China, you know. Are they for real sort of thing. We don't do missing persons.'

I nod and glance about the bar. This is not getting me very far. 'No missing persons. Right.'

'Hang on, when you say can we help you find someone, what exactly do you mean? Are you looking for someone specific, like a long lost friend from your Nanjing college days, or are you like aiming to find someone, you know, like a girl? Someone to chill out with when you're next in Beijing or something?'

'You do that?'

'There are websites for that sort of thing, man.'

'It's alright. That's not what I have in mind.'

'What is it then?'

I lean forward, ensuring Charlie doesn't overhear. Charlie's solution to my plight is that I should go to the police and report that my wife kidnapped my child. But I can't deal with all that drama and publicity. There's a guy at the office whose wife was accused of beating up their domestic helper. The bosses didn't like the negative publicity, and he's lucky they can't fire him outright, but his career has stalled. He's a local, too, which helps. Me, a foreigner, and black at that? They might claim they're short of good engineers. But I know there'll be very little protection when the crunch comes.

'Alex, it's like this, I need to find my family, but I need it done quiet-quiet. My wife, you see, she took my daughter and ran away . . .'

'Bloody hell!' He furrows his brow and takes a big swig of his beer. 'What the hell did you do?'

'It's a long story.'

'I bet it is. Somehow you don't quite strike me as a wife batterer. Jesus, I didn't even realize you were married, Chiponda.'

'I know they're in Shanghai. Kitty has relatives there. I've been there several times, checked around, but no one can help.'

'Police?'

'I've thought about it. No, no way. Not in China anyway. It's not like they've disappeared off the face of the earth. I know they're safe, so the cops won't even listen. She emails sometimes, you see. There's been the occasional phone call, but I don't believe it's her number. And it's always blocked, anyway.'

I look over his shoulders and see Charlie chatting up a girl at the end of the bar. He's holding her hand, inspecting her bracelet. Alex is staring at me as though I were an alien. I can see he's still reeling from that exchange with Charlie.

Through the clouds of smoke I see Obiako's tall figure making its way towards us. I try desperately to catch his eye and warn him to keep his big mouth shut. I'm too late.

'Hey, landowner!' He calls out, and gives me a big hug. 'How does it feel to turn from squatter to master, eh?'

I try to wave him away and struggle to keep a straight face. But inside I'm boiling. Alex peers at me over his beer. It seems he's recoiling from me. Perhaps it's just my imagination.

'What's this, man? What's he talking about?'

Before I can answer Alex, Obiako blurts out, 'You're looking at your new master, my good man. You'd better buy him a beer, and while you're at it, mine's a Tsingtao.' He bursts out laughing. I step on his toes and squeeze twice.

'You talk too much nonsense, Obiako.'

Alex is not convinced. He leans over so close I can smell his cologne, in spite of the cigarette smoke. 'What's he on about, man?'

'You're talking like you don't know the man, Alex.' I push Obiako aside and face Alex. 'I can't comment on this crap. Look, are you going to help or not? This is important.'

The suspicion still lurks in his eyes.

'Look, Chiponda, we've got this shit hovering over us, and you know what? I don't need it, frankly. I don't need it any more than you do. But you've got to be honest with me. Your family have overrun a farm, is that what Obiako's saying?'

'What does it matter, Alex? I've got a much bigger problem on my hands. The stuff going on back in Zim, your family, my family, Jesus Christ man, right now, I just want to get my wife and baby back here with me. If you can't help, just forget it!' I gulp down my beer and make my way to the door.

I can barely concentrate on my work all week. We're preparing a tender for a road rehabilitation project but there's a cloud hanging over the firm. It's rumoured that Ah Cheung, one of our directors, took bribes on a building construction project. The tension in the air is almost palpable. He was once cleared of a similar charge. They're sure to get him this time. The publicity won't do us any good.

My boss wants me to travel to Shanghai to talk to one of our big clients. This could be my chance.

In the late afternoon I get a text message from Lai-Mui. She wants to meet me after work. I suggest the Africa Oasis on Knutsford Terrace. I arrive twenty minutes early, at ten past six, and take a seat on the pavement beneath the overhead fans, where the humidity is manageable. There are people waiting for tables at some of the restaurants. If this is what it's like in an economic downturn, I wonder what it was like in the boom years of the eighties which I've heard so much about.

When Lai-Mui arrives I'm already on my second beer. She's in a smart dark suit and matching black shoes. After greetings she orders an orange juice.

'I can't stay long, Chiponda,' she says. 'My parents arrived from Vancouver yesterday. Two-week holiday. I'm meeting them for dinner.'

'I don't suppose I'll be getting invited to this dinner for a nice happy family gathering?'

'Chiponda. If it was up to me . . .'

'I'm sorry, Lai-Mui.' I squeeze her shoulder. 'It's just that, sometimes I feel I have nothing here. This whole place is just . . . a desert, since Kitty left.'

'I know. Any news from home, your family? I saw on TV last night. Terrible.'

I start to laugh, but not without unease. The news from Africa is forever predictable. And Lai-Mui's reaction is just typical. I'm thinking how she would react if I told her my family are now wealthy landowners, or maybe simply landowners. But this is no time for jokes. Lai-Mui has many questions in her eyes. I ask her what's wrong.

'I never really asked you before,' she says. 'It's none of my business, I know . . .'

'Lai-Mui, you're the only family I've got here. You can ask me anything.'

'Why did Kitty leave? I mean, I know what she told me . . .'

'What's my side of the story?' She nods.

'She wouldn't lie to you. Whatever she might have said, the money I lost gambling in Macau, the loan sharks harassing us, the threats, chicken entrails on the door, all that's true. What she never believed is about the girl. The girl who set me up, claiming she was getting freelance work for me. I was stupid, hanging out with her, believing her. But there was nothing between us. Kitty's never believed that.'

'I know the Tiffany story. Are you telling me the truth?'

'Lai-Mui, I swear upon my . . .'

'Don't, don't! It's bad luck.'

'Whatever it takes to make you believe.' She eyes me for a long, pensive moment. There's nothing more I can say. It feels as though my life is in her hands.

'It's the threats then, yeah? Harassment. She was scared. For Chacha.'

'I can fully understand her fear, Lai-Mui. But I paid them back. Every little penny. And they haven't needed to trouble me again. She won't believe me; why?'

She's agonizing over something. She looks into my eyes, glances at her watch, and then fixes her gaze on the people walking by. I leave her to her thoughts.

'Chiponda, I don't know if I should do this.'

I hold my breath. 'What is it?'

'Little Chacha . . . you can't imagine how I miss her. That night . . . never mind. I know Kitty will kill me. But, for a favourite niece . . . You were not supposed to know. She wants to see you, she misses you, but she's not sure. You only have to talk to her.'

Kitty wants to see me? 'What . . . when . . .'

'She's coming to see our parents. For just a day. They refused to fly to China.'

'She's coming? Chacha! What about Chacha?'

'Chacha's with relatives. She's fine. Kitty called me last night.

I spoke to my niece.'

I'm struggling not to jump from my seat. All these months. Waiting.

'Her flight arrives at 8.15 . . .'

I don't wait for her to finish her sentence. Quick kiss on her forehead and I'm flying down the road like a maniac, trying to flag down a cab.

The Lion's Tears

Nobody noticed them steal out of the dormitory. Everyone was preoccupied with their own activities. Some boys played cards, others played draughts with bottle tops on cardboards, but most just chatted, teased each other, told jokes. There was not much else to do after dinner. The main priority for Jesu Reformatory Home was to rescue homeless boys from the streets.

Finding things for twelve year olds to do in the evening would be worked out over time, as Teacher Joshua kept reminding anyone who asked.

'Wait here,' said Timothy, rushing back into the dormitory.

Minutes later, he reappeared, a timid-looking Kasala by his side. Mbatu glared at them in the semi-darkness. 'Where is he going? You know he can't . . .'

'Quiet. I'll explain later.'

'No, I want to know now,' said Mbatu. 'Are you forcing him?'

'He wants to come but he's not sure, so . . .'

'Ah! So you're his teacher now, eh? Kasala, do you want to go to Mama Mboga's or not?'

Kasala glanced at both Mbatu and Timothy as if wondering which one to trust.

'Hey! Talk!'

'I . . . I'm not going to drink anything. I'll just come and see.'

'It's alright, Kasala. Timothy won't force you to do anything.'

'So I can come?'

With a puzzled expression, Timothy turned to Kasala. But

103

Kasala was already walking towards the secret escape route behind the storerooms. A few minutes earlier, Mbatu had checked to ensure the security guard was fast asleep at the main gate. At the fence, they parted the barbed wire and glided away into the shadows. In the distance the lights of Nairobi city sparkled and enticed, reminding the boys how they once ended up there.

They trooped down a disused footpath on the other side of the fence, every so often casting a wary glance over their shoulders. The darkness was like a thick, black fog. The boys could barely see where they were going. There wasn't a soul in sight, and the only noise was that of maize plants rustling in the light wind. The abrupt hooting of an owl sent a chill down three spines. The boys came to a momentary stop. Then they moved on, groping through the darkness with their hands as though to ward off an unseen enemy. Only Timothy dared laugh at their fright. The moon was playing hide and seek, one minute sneaking behind the clouds and winking from the corners, and the next moment emerging as though to sneer at the three silhouettes scuttling away from the safety of the Home into the unknown. A few stars winked as though conniving in the boys' mischief.

Kasala's teeth clattered and his eyes bulged out to see the danger he believed lay ahead. He glanced back hopefully, but there was nothing to see there. He would never be able to find his way back by himself. This was the farthest he had ever ventured from the Home. A small voice told him he was letting Teacher Joshua down. But he convinced himself he had been coerced into going on this adventure. If Teacher found out, he would say it was Timothy's fault.

Yet a part of him was anxious to see what it was the others went to do at the slums on the outskirts of Nairobi. What was this chang'aa drink they kept talking about which was made from the tears of lions? Or this glue they sniffed which sent you flying to heaven? When he lived on the streets he stayed out of trouble and kept himself busy begging. When others talked of going 'flying' he turned and walked the other way.

'Okay, Timothy,' said Mbatu, breaking the long silence. 'Tell me how you persuaded Kasala to come out.'

'Easy. I said I would tell he claims he slept with that girl in the kitchen.'

'That's not fair.'

'Fair! You think our life is fair? Living in this stupid, boring Home, and we can't have the freedom we had in the streets. We can't even go look for our families . . .'

'Your family?' muttered Kasala. 'Look for them? You left them yourself!'

'Don't say that! You think I don't want to see my mother?'

'So why did you leave her?'

'You can't ask me that, Kasala! I was small, I don't know, I can't remember!'

'And why just your mother?' said Kasala, 'Why not your father, your brothers and sisters?'

'Hey, leave me alone!'

'Stop that,' said Mbatu. 'Can we just go and have some fun?'

Timothy cursed and spat into the darkness.

They arrived at the slum area of Korogocho and started to make their way through a narrow street. The slum district was illuminated by a reluctant moon and dim points of light along the streets which came from hurricane lamps and charcoal cooking stoves. Dogs barked. Children with distended stomachs played on the streets, squealing and chasing each other through the dark, narrow alleys that separated the hovels, carefully avoiding the dark piles of ordure that were barely visible in the semi-darkness. Babies cried. Adults argued. The sound of a woman singing a hymn stung the air. It sounded like a dirge, her voice rising and fading, then breaking, as though cowering with fear under the tyranny of the wind. The smell of maize-meal *ugali* filled the air.

In the semi-darkness the boys saw rows of wooden huts stacked up against each other as if to lend each other the strength to stand on the uneven ground. The only other people in the streets were drunks who staggered, cursed, sang about their cows and goats and keeled over to vomit on the nearest mud or cardboard wall.

A man in a thread-bare coat tottered towards the boys,

blocking their way. He staggered this way and that, then steadied himself against a wall. A dog walked up to him, sniffed at him and started to piss on his legs. The man cursed and swung his leg to kick the dog. But he lost his balance and fell to the ground, blocking the boys' way and vomiting in rhythmic spasms that rocked him so vigorously the boys thought he was going to die. Mbatu and Timothy squeezed their way past the trembling body.

Kasala stood still, as though paralyzed. He wanted to call out to his friends to wait for him but couldn't find his voice. Mbatu walked back and reached a hand out to him. Kasala grabbed it and quickly hopped over the man who was already snoring. Kasala raced to catch up with Timothy who was laughing at him. He aimed a punch at Timothy's ribs. Timothy ducked and Kasala went crashing into a wall. Someone inside fired off a volley of insults.

Kasala gazed at the huts, wondering how they managed not to collapse. But the huts appeared to have an indestructible will to hang on to the ground. The City Council often razed them to the ground, hoping to rid the city of illegal squatters. But as soon as the smoke cleared and the dust settled, the slums germinated and a busy, robust community grew, like weeds in the rainy season.

The three boys stopped in front of a green door and Mbatu led the way in, after a perfunctory knock on the door. The hut was surprisingly clean inside, and it was a relief to get away from the smells outside.

A warm fire burned in the middle of the room and a paraffin lantern on a small table in a corner provided just enough light. A heavily-built woman sat on a low gaturua stool. Her eyes seemed to glow in the dim light. She greeted the boys and studied their faces, her eyes lingering on each timid face as though she was examining some rare ingredients for a special brew. She went to the door, peeped outside and waved them to the single bed before resuming her seat.

Mbatu and Timothy did not need prompting. They fished into their pockets and put their money together. It had taken a long time to save fifteen shillings from their share of the sale of the vegetables and flowers they grew in the Home. Still, no words were uttered, but everybody seemed to know what to do. It was like a silent film. Kasala watched the ritual with fascination.

The woman reminded Timothy of his own mother, who also used to sell chang'aa, also known as machozi ya simba, the lion's tears, to raise the family. Every time he saw Mama Mboga, he was transported back to a life that had, over the years, gradually wafted away, like a mist at the break of dawn. He was only four when he left the slum in another part of the city, attracted to the city streets by the bright lights, the tall buildings and the promise of coins scattering like confetti into little eager hands.

Mama Mboga took the money and wrapped it in a dark blue handkerchief, which she inserted in the cleavage of her bosom. Then she rummaged under the bed and pulled out a jerry can and some empty aluminium cans. Kasala's earlier sense of trepidation began to assail him again. When Mama Mboga handed him a can he accepted it with such a sense of resignation that she was tempted to snatch it back and sell it to someone who appreciated the taste and potency of lion's tears.

'You have been here before,' said Mama Mboga, remembering Mbatu's unsmiling face.

'A long time ago,' said Timothy.

'You are so young.'

'But old enough to drink this stuff!' said Timothy, laughing. 'Like men.'

Mama Mboga chuckled. 'Men indeed. Yes, like men. But where are the real men in this land? Everyone's drinking it. How else can people like us eat? You're so young. It seems wrong. But if you can handle it, and you have the money . . . And if I don't sell it to you, you'll get it at my neighbour's. You chose me, and that's my blessing.'

'Don't worry about us,' said Mbatu. 'We can take care of ourselves.'

'Of course we can,' added Timothy. 'The problem is money. Expensive, you see.'

'Not just for you, my children. The way things are, you would think the end of the world was near. I ask you, what is this poverty that came upon us? Where did all this suffering come from, eh? This government! Only God can help us now.' She paused and laughed, a loud, hollow laugh that made Kasala shiver. Then she went quiet and her chin dropped into her chest, as though she was embarrassed by her outburst.

The boys sipped their drinks in silence. Timothy looked at Mama Mboga and saw his mother. He saw the pain etched on her face, and longed to see the face break into a smile. But Mama Mboga's face was just like his mother's. Stubbornly unsmiling.

'Before it was just one party, that Kanu,' Mama Mboga went on. She spoke as though to herself, oblivious of her young audience. 'Kanu was our father and mother, we were constantly told. These politicians! The father who gave his son a stone when he asked for bread. A snake when he asked for fish. I would rather my father gave me lion's tears to drink and forget my sorrows. Now they say there are other parties. They're calling it democracia. It sounds like a disease to me. This government! Tell me, who left this curse of poverty upon our heads?'

'That's too bad,' said Mbatu, after glancing about him to see if the others wanted to respond. He could not imagine the hut without the sadness which seemed as real as the hard sisal mattress they sat on or the fire that cast dancing shadows on the walls.

'Yes, very sad,' echoed Timothy, recalling his mother's constant moaning about the problems of bringing up six children on her own. His father was hardly ever there. And when he came home late in the evening, all he wanted to do was drink her lion's tears. She asked him to support his children or pay for the drink. His response was to punch and kick her and the children, growling like an enraged lion.

Mama Mboga was not listening. Her gaze was fixed on the fire.

Kasala had hardly touched his drink. The few sips he had already taken had persuaded him that neither Teacher Joshua nor heaven would ever forgive him. The cackling fire mocked him, reminding him that he would forever burn in hell for his sins. The taste of the lion's tears set his tongue on fire, but he summoned enough courage to swallow the hot fluid. He choked and almost screamed as it burned his throat but immediately relaxed when it warmed his stomach and made his head feel light, as if a weight had been lifted off it.

Kasala noted with envy how Mbatu and Timothy seemed completely at ease. He studied their faces to understand how they could possibly enjoy drinking the lion's tears. To him it was like torture.

The noisy rumble of a drunk man made everyone look up. There was a knock on the door, followed by a gruff, unsteady voice: 'Mama Mboga! Mama Mboga, are you in, woman?'

'Come in, Baba Nimu.'

A shadowy figure appeared, completely covering the narrow doorway. Mama Mboga indicated a stool near the door. But the man ignored her. Staggering in and cursing, he slumped onto the bed, just next to Kasala. Kasala winced and held his breath. He glanced at his friends and saw Mbatu staring blankly into his lion's tears as though he expected some revelation from the colourless liquor.

Timothy glanced about him, the way the boys at the Home did when an argument started to get out of hand and they looked forward to a good fight. He watched the man closely, saw the wrinkles on the face, the unkempt beard, the graying hair. The broken nails had turned an ugly gray-brown. In his mind's eye he saw the sinewy hand curled around a tin cup. Teary eyes peered at him over the cup. When he asked his father what he was drinking, the man gulped down the fiery liquid and threw the tin cup at him, leaving a deep cut above the left eye. The memory faded. It was too long ago. Nothing was clear.

'Ai! Baba Nimu,' said Mama Mboga, 'the world is really coming to an end.'

'Ag! Nonsense! What world! Your world—*hic*—Mama Mboga, not mine! Not mine, if I'm—*hic*—the father of Nimu. Hey!' He let out a stream of coarse invectives, waving a hand above his head, slumped across the bed and soon started to snore.

Kasala's neck was buried in his shoulders, like a chicken watching a hawk gliding back and forth across the barn. Mama Mboga shifted her gaze from the snoring man slumped in a foetal position to the fire which had begun to die down. She looked into the fire and recalled the fires that occasionally wiped out the whole slum village. The fire burned with a determined fury for a minute, then the yellow and orange flames grew shorter. The dancing shadows they cast on the walls went still, as though exhausted by their dance. A twig cracked with a sound that was surprisingly loud in the quiet room. A yellow flame made a desperate leap, rose three inches and then disappeared into the gray ashes. There was nothing left of the fire but a dull, red glow.

Mama Mboga reached out to rekindle the fire, then changed her mind and snatched her hand away. The expression on her face was that of someone watching the end of her own life. Her heart beat faster as she recalled the fire in the slum. The smoke and heat woke her up. Children were screaming with terror. The whole village was crying for help. The air was filled with smoke, the smell of burning timber, and the burning flesh of young ones trapped in their slumber. The next day the property developers sent their bulldozers to clear the site, under the watchful gaze of City Council guards.

Timothy finished his drink, and shot a glance at Kasala who continued to grimace every time he took a tentative sip, like a child forced to take medicine. Timothy couldn't wait to get away from Baba Nimu's loud snores, but as his mind got lighter, he visualized his father lying on the dirt floor, telling tales of cows and goats he believed he owned. Then he and his siblings heard the tales of the great war, the one their father called the struggle for freedom. But even as Timothy marveled at the achievements of the freedom fighters, the struggle for freedom always paled in comparison with his father's struggle to rise from the floor onto the threadbare mattress on a rickety bed.

He studied the man's long fingers, and saw them reaching out to slap his face. Too long ago. He was too small. Another slum, somewhere else. But homes were destroyed. Hovels flattened by unforgiving bulldozers whose drivers stared ahead, as though under the spell of their rumbling machines. People moved on, turned into refugees in their own city. Children succumbed to the allure of the streets. Men abandoned their families. Women sold vegetables. And lion's tears. And their bodies.

'I'll finish this for you,' said Mbatu, reaching for Kasala's drink. He took two gulps and passed it on to Timothy. Kasala sighed with relief.

'Mama Mboga,' said Baba Nimu, waking up with a start. 'Have they come today?' He tried to sit up but ended up collapsing on Kasala who screamed and then covered his mouth in shame.

'Last week. They took everything.'

'Poured away?'

'Every little drop. It made a river. A large river, like all the lions of the world crying. They don't understand it is our life.'

She paused, realizing the man had fallen asleep again. Even in the semi-darkness, the boys could not fail to see the points of light in her wide-open eyes.

'Mama Mboga,' Baba Nimu called out, 'I'm thirsty!'

'Not on credit again, Baba Nimu. I have to make a living.'

'Ag! You'll get your—*hic*—money tomorrow, woman.'

'That's what you always say. And now you owe me a hundred shillings.'

Baba Nimu laughed and swallowed hard. He searched one pocket after another. They all watched him as though he was a street entertainer, anxious not to miss his next trick. Mama Mboga breathed a sigh of relief when he extracted a crumpled twenty shilling note from his shirt pocket and thrust it into her hands. Timothy smiled to himself.

'I told you! I told you I pay for my drink!'

'Thank you.' Mama Mboga fetched under the bed for the jerry can.

Baba Nimu's grin showed tobacco-stained brown teeth. He looked down at the boys and asked who they were. The boys introduced themselves. Baba Nimu furrowed his brow and studied Timothy's face intensely.

'How old are you, boy?'

'Twelve, I guess.' They gazed into each other's eyes. Baba Nimu scratched his head and pursed his lips. He turned to look at the dying embers and held his can of lion's tears so tightly the bones seemed about to break through the dry wrinkled skin.

'Twelve, eh?'

He fished out a half-smoked cigarette from a breast pocket, then bent down to pick up an ember from the fire. But he lost his balance and his body slumped forward. His lion's tears went flying into the fire, causing the dying embers to sputter into life.

Everyone gasped and instinctively reached out to save him. Timothy and Mbatu got to him first, but the brown jacket brushed against the fire and started to burn. Mama Mboga snatched a bowl from a side table, dipped it into a barrel of water and doused the burning jacket. The two boys held Baba Nimu between them to stop him falling again.

Baba Nimu's eyes were like those of a man who had narrowly missed being hit by a bus. He scanned the faces of the two boys and shook his head. He kept muttering 'Twelve years! Twelve years! Such a long time.' He started to cry. The sobs rocked his body like epileptic spasms. Timothy stared into the dying fire, struggling hard not to blink and fighting the tears that collected in his eyes.

Without warning, Baba Nimu lurched forward and vomited in the fireplace. Timothy and Mbatu still held his arms. Mama Mboga poured herself a cup of lion's tears. She shifted her gaze from Timothy to Baba Nimu, and her face started to break into a smile. But it was a smile tinged with regret, as though she had found a long lost treasure that she no longer had any use for. Her face was like the calm, smooth surface of the earth after the floods had gone, washing the litter and garbage away.

Mbatu saw the smile and followed her eyes. And then he too noticed the resemblance. He nodded to himself and stared unseeing at the red embers and the blue smoke that rose slowly to the rafters on which Mama Mboga kept her firewood and often hid jerry cans of lion's tears.

Timothy looked up to see Kasala standing at the door. He swallowed hard, took out his handkerchief and wiped Baba Nimu's face. When he got up to leave, he took a final look behind him. The smile in Mama Mboga's eyes urged him to stay on. He breathed hard, and raised his hand to wave goodbye. He saw Baba Nimu holding the handkerchief against his cheek like a treasured memento, eyes open wide, like those of a rabbit held up by its ears, unable to move. Timothy remembered those eyes well, as he listened to the tales of the cows and the goats he now knew his father never had. He heard the cries of his mother and siblings, as their father lashed out in their tiny hovel, kicking, punching, laughing drunkenly, looking for the hidden jerry cans.

He stumbled out, supporting himself against Mbatu.

'What's the matter with you?' asked Kasala as they made their way through the deserted street. 'She reminds you so much of your mother?'

'You're so blind, Kasala,' muttered Mbatu.

Timothy could barely see through his tears.

And then the End

They came for him last night. Bundled him into a police van with a black hood over his head as though he was some common criminal, or a homeless immigrant. They wouldn't give him face. After everything he has done for them, everything he has given them.

Even the police vans they drove up in. He gave them to the city. Every single one of them. If it was up to me I would have had them locked up, purged, their families too, and their homes razed to the ground, till they turned as black as coal.

The city's chief of police was on the news this morning. There was a time I revered the man, admired him for his courage and sense of duty. Did he not tackle the gangs of hoodlums that once terrorized people near Shinhuan Railway Station? Conning travellers, robbing old women of their crumpled yuan notes. He cleaned it up. The city knew then that he was a true comrade of the people.

But after the words he spoke this morning, it has all changed for me. *We'll catch every little rat that's feeding off the people,* he growled, mistakenly believing he was a tiger. He might have the paws and teeth, but wouldn't know what to do with the grace and honour if he had them. The police boss is a man with a short memory. Guan Fuzhan paid for his son's education in America. But does any of that matter now? They're saying the city bosses are leaning on him to act. But how can he so easily forget the happiness he has indulged in, the generous gifts he has accepted over the years, like a son favoured by a benevolent father who asks for nothing but gratitude?

The police chief is just shining the shoes of the party and city top brass. He wants to silence a few big voices to divert attention from his declining popularity. That's the logic that lives in his head, saying lock them up, show them who's boss. And yet it is people like Guan Fuzhan who made him what he is today. Shinhuan wouldn't be the prosperous city it is if it wasn't for far-sighted investors like Guan Fuzhan.

～

As I drive to pick up the boys from their golf lesson I spot the Mayor's motorcade. Going to some function. Perhaps another press conference where he'll release more details about this shocking purge.

Two of the BMWs in the motorcade were donated by Guan Fuzhan. Only last year. They welcomed him, sang his praises, spoke in glowing terms about his dedication to the city. His love of the people. They've forgotten all those colourful words, all that praise and love they showered on him. I should have guessed. It was just talk, devoid of sincerity. Now they talk of economic crimes. The death penalty. Such grim words.

The two boys are struggling to go about their lives as if nothing has happened. That's the way it should be. Having been born abroad and seeing the world has made them strong. I try not to listen to their conversation but their words fill the space in the limousine, squeezing out the dull voice on the radio. Personally I don't care much for the radio. But Guan Fuzhan always likes to have it on. That way he knows the city is keeping track of his good deeds, appreciating the way he continues to shape the city. But today it's a different story, it's all praises for the mayor and police chief for taking tough action. *Tough action!* My mouth fills with bile. I turn the radio off. For the boys. They're just teenagers. They shouldn't have to listen to this. I know how much they adore their father. Their whispers betray fear, the uncertainty of what the future holds for their tender lives that are only just unfolding. Oh, the joys of youth.

'We shouldn't be out like this.'

'Like what?'

'Out playing golf, as if everything's the same.'

'Everything's the same.'

'It's not! We should be with mother, comforting her.'

'Don't worry, she'll be alright.'

'Do you think they'll . . .' I glance at the mirror. A meaningful look, face creased with a scowl of terror. He shouldn't be thinking such thoughts. Such a young boy. It can't come to that. It won't come to that.

'Shh!' A shake of the head. So thoughtful. He remembers the elderly man, who is not supposed to be privy to the family woes. If only he knew. But it is better like this.

'I'm afraid if they . . .'

'They won't, alright? Don't imagine such evil thoughts.'

'But father said . . .'

'Forget what father said. We have to be strong now, for mother.'

But the terror remains. Even on the older boy's face. He always tries to look tough. It's what their father teaches them. He'll do well. He'll make his father proud. It's their mother I'm worried about. She's a business partner, involved as much as the father. Everyone expects her to go down too. Perhaps they're trying to protect a woman's honour. They hold up half the sky after all, the women.

The boys remain silent. They never talk to me. They never notice me. I exist only on the edges of their consciousness. I like it like that. That way I can watch over them in silence. They know so little about me. But who am I to complain? I'm just a driver. That's what they think. Because that's what they see. They'll never know their little auntie, my niece, who is looked after by their father. Mei's apartment is just half a mile away from their house. If anything happens to Guan Fuzhan, my poor niece could be in trouble. I truly hope he has provided for her, and her one-year old daughter. Such a lovely little child. What sort of world will she grow into? She's lucky Guan Fuzhan is her father. But the boys must never know. And certainly not their mother. She's a good woman, to her sons at least. But she would never accept Mei.

≈

It has been a week since the arrest. The family's falling apart. Word reached Guan Fuzhan's wife that they were planning to come after her. She left last night, with the two boys. I drove them to the airport. I can only hope they're safe wherever they are. Now that I don't have to drive, I can listen to the radio, and watch the news round the clock, fishing for information. I stay at home all day. I can't return to the village, in case Guan Fuzhan is released and needs me to pick him up.

The news comes five days later. It's just a small item, sandwiched between stories of criminals, real criminals, the type that rob banks with AK47 guns. Such a small item I could easily have missed it. It comes early in the morning, as my wife steams dumplings for breakfast. *Investigations into graft and embezzlement in Shinhuan have been completed.* It takes me a while to realize what the announcer is talking about. She has a calm, expressionless face, the same expression with which she reports on bank robbers and pick-pockets. This is the same young woman who has made a career of reporting Guan Fuzhan's great deeds. How everything's changed.

Something inside me snaps. The walls are going round and round in a mad dance. Memories flash through my mind. The fifteen years I've worked for Guan Fuzhan. From the early days when he opened his first shop and owned an old decrepit car that growled and farted with a grim determination when you turned the ignition. I lived through the changing fortunes in his business world, going from car to car, and each one a better, more powerful and more elegant statement of Guan Fuzhan's status. He is a generous and kind boss, the perfect son in law. I'm unlucky it never crossed his mind to ask for my daughter. She would have been so much better off with a man like him. Now she's stuck with that good for nothing government clerk who can't see the world beyond his desk.

'Completed!' exclaims my wife, looking up. I didn't even know she was paying attention to the news. I'm surprised she can hear the sound of the TV above the sizzling noises from her wok. But her kitchen is small, and she stands in front of the gas cooker, her back to the space we call the dining room. She turns her head to face me. 'What do they mean, *lougong*?'

What can I tell her? What is there to tell? The TV station itself does not deem it necessary to go into the gory details. It's their idea of protecting public morality.

'It's finished. It's the end, *loupor*.'

My teeth press against my lip, hard, as if wanting to exact revenge. But for what?

'The end? What is this end?'

How can I protect her from the knowledge of the fate that awaits Guan Fuzhan? It is the kind of thing we can whisper about in the square outside, where old people like us while the time away playing music and going through their ballroom dance routine. But in the flat? I look into my wife's eyes, her face tormented by worry and the fear that tears through my insides even more keenly than hers. The thought of a son being taken away from us. For he truly was like the son we never had. He showed me respect, always asked after my family, gave generous gifts.

It's the end. My wife knows it. There'll be no more reports on the news. There'll be a court case, a hurried affair. And then the end.

The dumplings don't taste the same. It's not *loupor*'s fault. She has done everything right, like she always does. They're soft, gentle on the mouth. But my tongue refuses to recognize the spicy and sour taste, the smooth texture, not even the light soy sauce that trickles down their sides, turning the white surface a dark brown that reminds me of cough syrup.

'Does it not trouble you, *lougong*? The things the big men do?' I glare at my wife. But she's undaunted. She goes on, placing a plate of *ha gau* on the table. 'The things they do. When is it enough? Does a time come when you say my stomach is full now, take the food away?'

'Have you considered these could be lies from jealous enemies?'

'Ha! You'll believe whatever they tell you, the fool they've made you.'

My breakfast unfinished, my wife's sharp words still ringing in my ears, I make my way to the temple near the public square. They'll have some answers there.

The temple will share its secrets. The air in the courtyard fills with the smell of joss sticks and incense, drawing me inside. I approach, with slow, soundless steps. Head bowed in reverence to the Most Benevolent Deity, I shake the bundle of fortune sticks, until one falls out. I memorize the number, match it to a list of the Ancient Sacred Poems and approach a fortune teller outside. Yau Kau Bit Ying.

The sign on the wall whispers its solemn message. Ask in earnest, you shall receive.

The words she utters glide past my ears, like a breeze without a message, a mosquito buzzing an empty promise. For it is wisdom I yearn for. Wisdom to understand what it was Guan Fuzhan did wrong, and my little niece, what has she too done wrong, to have been thrust into such an unlikely life and is now on the verge of being plucked away so cruelly.

The end that my wife asked about speaks so loudly, so irreversibly, for Guan Fuzhan. But the questions remain, not asked, hardly understood, never answered. Like the doubt that gnaws at my heart, inexorably, as if to parcel out my share of a punishment for a crime to which I didn't even realize I was complicit. Until the end.

Acknowledgements

Grateful acknowledgment is made for permission to reprint from the following: *New York Stories* for 'The Smell of Fresh Grass'; *Ambit Magazine* for 'Private Lessons'; *Wasafiri* for 'The Dream Went Out'; *Dreams, Miracles and Jazz* for 'Random Check'; *Kunapipi* for 'Black Fishnet Stockings'; *Author-me* for 'The Warrior's Last Job' and 'The Lion's Tears'; and *Havenbooks* for 'For a Favourite Niece'.

There are many people whose support I would like to acknowledge, in particular my late father who walked a wide-eyed seven-year old into a high school library and opened up a wondrous world that has never lost its allure; uncle Kamau who declared to a class of bewildered class six kids that his nephew was writing a storybook; pity they've waited so long; mum for life and love; the numerous editors who believed in these stories; and Jen Hamilton-Emery for giving this collection a chance to breathe.

Printed in the United Kingdom
by Lightning Source UK Ltd.
133968UK00001B/94-99/A